WHERE WILL WE GO?

# WHERE WILL WE GO?

## A Sequel

Emily Craig

NEW DEGREE PRESS

WHERE WILL WE GO?
*A Sequel*

ISBN

978-1-63730-679-6   *Paperback*

978-1-63730-768-7   *Kindle Ebook*

979-8-88504-038-9   *Digital Ebook*

*To my sweet angel, my Nanny, Jean Casteel.*

*June 23, 1941–April 25, 2021*

# CONTENTS

---

A NOTE FROM THE AUTHOR                                    11

PREFACE                                                   15


CHAPTER 1    TO PARIS, MY DEAR?                            17

CHAPTER 2    SO CLOSE                                      29

CHAPTER 3    LET'S JET!                                    39

CHAPTER 4    BONJOUR, FRIENDS                              47

CHAPTER 5    PARIS AWAITS                                  53

CHAPTER 6    EIFFEL TOWER                                  61

CHAPTER 7    A VIEW FROM THE TOP                           69

CHAPTER 8    CEMETERY TRIP                                 77

CHAPTER 9    THE LOUVRE                                    87

CHAPTER 10   THE BERRY'S                                   93

CHAPTER 11   APPROACHING DEADLINE                         101

CHAPTER 12   RODIN MUSEUM                                 109

CHAPTER 13   FIRST TRAVEL ARTICLE                         119

CHAPTER 14   WINE CELEBRATION              123

CHAPTER 15   WALL OF LOVE                  133

CHAPTER 16   SECOND TRAVEL ARTICLE         143

CHAPTER 17   THE FINAL ADVENTURE           147

CHAPTER 18   SAYING GOODBYE                157

CHAPTER 19   HELLO AMERICA                 165

CHAPTER 20   THIRD TRAVEL ARTICLE          173

CHAPTER 21   FOURTH TRAVEL ARTICLE         177

CHAPTER 22   PARTY TIME                    181

CHAPTER 23   DECEMBER REVEALS              193

CHAPTER 24   UNEXPECTED                    203


EPILOGUE                   215

ACKNOWLEDGMENTS            221

*"Until you spread your wings, you will have no idea how far you can fly."*

—NAPOLEON BONAPARTE

# A NOTE FROM THE AUTHOR

———

*"Maybe there's something you're afraid to say, or someone you're afraid to love, or somewhere you're afraid to go. It's gonna hurt. It's gonna hurt because it matters."*

—JOHN GREEN

Dear Readers,

I choose to rise above all the pain.

I wrote this book during a very dark and confusing time in my life. Two years after a major heartbreak, I found myself still triggered by internal failure. I felt lost and hopeless. Writing had always been my escape, my oasis from the world. I leaned into it and embedded my deepest and darkest moments into Lucy's world. She is my vessel of hope and light. My saving grace when I see no way out of my own torment.

I want to share stories of hope with you to show you that hope is possible after any heartbreak in your life. This book is for the happy, sad, successful, failure, adventurous soul, romantic, and heartbroken person out there in the world. No matter what struggle or exciting moment you are facing, this book is for every moment. Life is beautiful and messy—cherish every bit.

Heartbreak comes in many shapes and forms throughout our lives, but it doesn't have to take you down with it. You can either rise above or give in.

In my debut book *Will You Love Me Again?* Lucy's husband cheated on her. Although I have never been cheated on, I knew what it felt like to have everything turned upside-down in a split second. I started to question why I wasn't enough for my ex-boyfriend, even though I was miserable in that relationship. I found an outlet to express my deepest darkest feelings in *Where Will We Go?* That, in turn, helped me grow and heal.

I didn't handle my breakup with a positive mindset. Lucy experiences the pain, then slowly comes to terms with her new beginning. But her heartbreak wasn't her final chapter, and neither was mine. We both had a lot to learn in our lives and needed closure and more chapters.

While writing this book, I faced my biggest demons—the way my ex used to make me feel, our memories, and our devastating ending. I drew on the pain and forced myself to not back down from the ache his very name brought me. After two years, he was still controlling my thoughts, but I finally said no more and began writing a new story—my story. Although this book is fiction, I weave in parts of my heartbreak trauma.

In 2021, I can say I am free. After facing my pain for what it was, heartbreak, I found love again.

Before I found my forever love, I struggled with wanting to make new connections such as friends or a relationship after having my heart shattered multiple times. Those wants, needs, and desires of having something new were pushed to the back burner. They became emotions farfetched. Instead of bottling up my hurt, I wanted to build a narrative that showed the aftermath of an earth-shattering heartbreak. I felt compelled to invite people to see the good and ugly parts of healing and finding yourself. For a long time, I didn't feel comfortable with the healing process because I had to realize that my healing timeline wasn't the same as anyone else's. I had to learn how to accept my growth and keep pushing forward even when the world around me kept telling me to hurry up and bounce back. As if I were a robot trained to only experience emotions for a limited time, but I'm human, and healing doesn't work that way. Healing is a process that requires time, growth, reflection, and acceptance.

Our world paints a terrible picture of heartbreak, so paint a different picture. "Dream a better dream," as Max says in *The Adventures of Sharkboy and Lavagirl.* Your life doesn't suddenly stop, even if it seems like you are standing still. I promise there is hope after your heart shatters.

Heartbreak is a season in life when we can explore ourselves and the world around us. The aftermath is only the first stepping-stone, so how you handle that life change will say a lot about your strength and ambition.

My story wasn't over. Heartbreak was never my curtain call. Maybe it was my beginning.

My wish is for Lucy to be a symbol of hope and growth. If nothing else, she'll provide strength through whatever heartbreak you may be going through.

Embrace the pain.


With Love,
Em

# PREFACE

———

## AUGUST 16, 2021

Two years of marriage ruined by one drunken mistake.

At the young age of twenty-two, fresh out of college, I married my high school sweetheart. Our life together was perfect, too perfect. We fell into sync effortlessly.

Trouble rose to the surface faster than either of us expected or asked for after saying "I do" in June 2018. Only two years later, my then-husband, David Lee, went to a bar with his high school buddies. After too many drinks, a woman came up behind him and started flirting. David slipped his ring into his pocket, took the woman's hand, and went home with her.

I didn't find out for almost a week. In a heated fight on June 2, 2020, I kicked him out of our house. A few months later, I broke my silence with my best friend, Jenny Thompson Morgan, and spilled the beans on what went down with David. She urged me to do what was best for me and that she thought he was a jerk.

We needed a guy's opinion. I reached out to Michael Sparks, one of my friends from college. He reminded me that cheating isn't acceptable, and I shouldn't have to wait around to see if he did it again. *Do your heart a favor and file for divorce before it gets worse, he said.*

In August 2020, I filed for divorce from my high school sweetheart. A year later, he announced his engagement to the woman who ended our marriage.

# CHAPTER 1

# TO PARIS, MY DEAR?

---

## AUGUST 16–17, 2021

I sit cross-legged in my comfy chair on an atypical August afternoon. My divorce is final. My ex-husband is engaged to his mistress. I still can't believe this is my life.

Yesterday, I promised my best friend, Jenny, that I would call her. Picking up my phone, I tap her contact in my favorites list and listen for her voice. As soon as the dial tone connects, I spill my guts.

"Jenny, did I ever tell you that I wanted to travel someday? I know I told Michael, but I can't remember if I told you."

After all these years, two of my best friends are meeting in person. Jenny and I are childhood best friends. Michael and I met while we were studying professional writing in college. Their paths in person haven't crossed yet, but that is all about to change when I reveal my travel plans. I can barely contain my excitement.

"Lucy, breathe for a minute, goodness. No, you haven't told me."

I gleefully scream, "I will tell you now, then!"

"Hurry up and tell me, girl!"

"Okay, so last year, Michael and I were talking about dream places we wanted to travel to because he was telling me about his travel plans. I have been thinking more about it. Since the divorce is now final, I want to spread my wings and venture out into the world. What do you think?"

"I think this is a great idea. Two questions. Are you taking me? And can we also invite Michael? I want to officially meet the guy who single-handedly helped you divorce that jerk of an ex-husband."

I gasp. "Jenny!"

"Sorry, but he was a jerk. Michael swooped in like a prince."

I shake my head. Leave it to my best friend to dis my ex and praise my college best friend in the same sentence.

"I know, but still no dissing. Oh, that's right, I still have to introduce y'all. Oops!"

"I enjoy dissing cheaters."

"Don't we all?"

She laughs, then asks, "But, the more important thing is, how have you managed to keep Michael hidden all these years?"

"Michael hasn't come to Athens since my wedding. He left right after congratulating me and talking for a bit. You were off taking care of your maid of honor duties. A while after the wedding, we met up in Florence, but not since that dinner."

"So, you are saying I missed meeting your awesome friend?"

"Exactly. But now the opportunity is upon us, and we have to take it."

"Yes, we do!" Jenny prompts me. "So, where are we venturing off to then?"

"I landed the travel writer position with *Getaway Travel Magazine*," I squeal. "How do you feel about Paris?"

Michael interned for *Getaway Travel Magazine* during his senior year in college, the fall semester after my June wedding. He was in Los Angeles for an entire term. He inspired me to apply for a permanent position with their magazine. The last I heard, he was working on writing short horror stories and poems. I can't wait to catch up with him.

"Wait. Did you say Paris? Like *the* Paris, France? Your favorite city? I say yes! Best-friend adventure is definitely a yes! I am so happy for you!"

"A much-needed best friend vacation!"

"We need to clue Michael in," she laughs. "Wait, when do they want you to leave?"

"Next week. Are you teaching any classes this semester?"

Jenny was barely out of college when she landed her first assistant teaching job in the history department at our local community college. In utter disbelief, she immediately started working and slowly worked her way up over the next two years. Last year, she received the title "History Professor." Working year-around, I'm not sure she is free to take off for four weeks.

"That is so soon! No, I actually wanted to take the semester off. Good timing, huh?"

"Very good timing. I'm one lucky girl. So meet tomorrow?"

"Sounds good to me. I think we are both lucky. The getaway of a lifetime."

"Here's to getting out of the country. I'll make a group chat so we can discuss times and places."

"Ah, I am so excited!"

"Me too! I'll text you."

"Talk to you soon, bye!"

"Talk then. Bye."

*Besties Group Chat*

Me: Hey y'all! So, Jenny already knows this, sorry, Michael. I landed the travel writer position at *Getaway Travel Magazine* (yes, same as your internship), and my first assignment is this month. They are helping me with expenses. This is a paying job. More details to come. Michael, are you free to meet up with Jenny and me tomorrow afternoon in Athens? By the way, you're coming with us to Paris.

Me: It is time to dip into your savings, y'all!

Michael: Ha ha, thanks for clueing me in, y'all. No hard feelings. Tomorrow's perfect. Where and what time?

Jenny: What about we grab lunch at noon. Where do y'all want to eat?

Me: Y'all know I am always down for food.

Michael: If food wasn't involved, it wouldn't be your meeting. Also, Jenny, we finally get to meet. I'm stoked!

Jenny: Michael, you are so right! Luce is made of food. Yes, finally time to meet. Sorry, we haven't met in person yet.

Me: All right, all right, I love food. We know. Yes, finally, I let my two best friends meet. What sounds good from this list: Samurai, Applebee's, or Cracker Barrel?


Connecting my Bluetooth to my car radio, I click on the *My Jams* Spotify playlist and start singing "Old Me" by 5 Seconds of Summer at the top of my lungs as I pull onto the road. I tap the steering wheel and cheerily make my way to Highway 72.

I wasn't always this way. Life was hard after the divorce. Six months finalized, and I can finally say I am happy about my brunette curls that fall around my face—the way he used to love it, my ex. But that doesn't matter anymore. I let the wave of nostalgia pass.

Twenty minutes later, I pull into Samurai's parking lot and take a spot close to the door. I look for Michael's navy Jeep and Jenny's baby-blue GMC Terrain, and I come up empty. Panicking, I send them a text.

Me: I'm parked by the door. Where are y'all?

I check the parking lot as my phone vibrates in the cupholder.

Jenny yells, "Hey, Luce!"

"Hey, Jen!" I yell back. "Where are you?"

Jenny taps on my window, making me jump.

Her flower-patterned sundress blows in the breeze. She presses her face to the window and says through the phone, "Come on!" She is effortlessly beautiful with bright green eyes and wavy brunette hair pinned up in a messy bun.

Jenny opens my door right after the lock pops up.

"Why, thank you, best friend." I smile and give her a small side hug. She is wearing my tan booties. I had almost forgotten I lent her those last week for her date night with Aaron. "Let's go get a table while we wait to hear from Michael."

The hostess leads us to a table in the front dining area. "Is a booth okay?"

Michael: I am outside. Where are y'all?

I cover my mouth and giggle. I say, "Oh, crap! We forgot to text him we were going inside."

"I guess we better tell him," Jenny says.

Jenny: Hey, sorry. I surprised Lucy at her car, and we completely forgot to send a text. Come on in. We are at a booth right inside the door.

Michael: On my way.

Seconds later, Michael walks in the door. I throw my hand up and wave him over to our booth. His jet-black hair falls in his face, probably overdue for a trim, and hits the top of his black rim glasses. He is sporting his favorite color today. A white baseball tee with royal blue quarter-sleeves, paired with faded black jeans, and black lace-up Converse.

Michael apologizes as he slides in next to me. "Sorry, it took me so long!"

"Boi, it is all good! You know I understand. We both do. Jenny used to drive to Florence all the time to see me. Didn't you, Jen?"

"Anything for you, Luce." She smiles. "Hi, Michael, I'm Jenny. It is nice to *finally* meet you." She draws the *finally* out while giving me a look.

I hold my hands up in surrender. "I apologize for not making this epic meeting happen sooner."

Michael looks me directly in the eye and says, "I forgive you, but I think Jenny will take some persuading."

Jenny grins back and says, "Yeah, you will really have to persuade me, like, a trip to Paris?"

"*That,* I can do!"

Michael says, "All right, Lucy, spill the beans on Paris!"

"Hold your horses."

"I don't know what horses you are speaking of." He nudges me and winks.

"Sure you don't, Sparks." I nudge him back. "Let's get down to business, shall we?"

"Are you going to start singing Disney tunes now?" Jenny asks.

They both roll their eyes.

"Hmm, no, not at all. No *Mulan* today."

"Good!" Michael reassures me. "Not that I don't love Disney tunes, but I would rather hear about Paris."

"I second that!" Jenny says. "What's the game plan, Luce?"

"I started researching flights, food, hotels, and potential places last night after our phone call. I even emailed my editor my article pitches. No response yet, but I am hoping I hear back soon."

"Well, what have you come up with?" Jenny asks, trying to keep me focused.

"Oh, right." I open my wallet purse and grab my list. "I have quite the list here. Are y'all ready? Information overload time!" I slide the papers over and start my spiel. "Okay, so we are flying out of Huntsville at 11:02 a.m. on August 24. We have two stops, the first in Atlanta, the second in Germany. We will arrive in Paris at 11:10 a.m. on August 25. Are y'all following?" I stop to catch my breath.

"That is a long flight." Michael gives me a puzzled look. "Why are they so specific?"

"The flight there is seventeen hours and eight minutes, but flying back home takes twenty hours and twenty-three minutes, with two different stops as well." I see their eyes get big. "*Guys*, we have a layover between stops. I think specific is their specialty, just like me."

Michael nods. "Ah, makes sense."

"Well," Jenny says, "we can say it is a trip worth taking because it *is* Paris, right?"

"I don't see why not!" I clap my hands and smile.

A few moments later, I take a couple of bites of my food before diving back into my Paris information overload. "*Getaway Travel Magazine* has most of the expenses covered, and we only need money for the extra stuff. They sent me just enough money for y'all's plane tickets and the hotel. They're sending me a company credit card, our plane tickets, and hotel information."

"That sounds like a dream come true," Michael says after taking a sip of his sweet tea.

Jenny says, "I agree. It must be a dream come true for you, Luce, our very own dreamer."

"It's a trip of a lifetime, and I am not taking it for granted." I clap my hands. "Back to planning. We are staying at the Cler Hotel, which is around a mile from the Eiffel Tower!"

Their jaws fall open.

"That close?" Jenny asks. "You're kidding."

"One second." I fumble with my phone then search on Google: *how close is Cler Hotel to the Eiffel Tower.* "Ah, here we go! By car, eight minutes away, but let's see the walking distances." I click the person on the direction screen, and it brings up three routes. I turn the phone around and point to the routes. "See, thirteen to fifteen minutes, and the shortest distance is a single kilometer."

"Wait, back up. What is that in miles?" Michael raises his eyebrow.

"Let me check." I go back to Google. "Under a mile, point six-two miles, to be precise."

"Not bad."

"As close to the Eiffel Tower as possible is how I like it."

Jenny says, "You've dreamed of going to Paris since... what, middle school?" She turns to Michael. "Did *she* tell you how long she's wanted to travel to Paris?"

"No!" He turns to me and says, "You've been holding out on me, girl!"

I hold my hands up in surrender. "Sometimes I can be forgetful, you know?"

Jenny says, "Wow, that's like hardly ever!"

"Fine. Fine." I huff. "I'm not a forgetful person, happy?"

"Very!" She laughs. "Now tell him the reason."

"Okay, okay. Promise you won't laugh?" I give him my best puppy dog eyes.

"Aren't you adorable?"

I sternly say, "Not the point. Do you promise?"

"I promise," he quickly vows.

"Do you remember the show *Pretty Little Liars*?"

"That show about a stalker named A?"

"The one and only." My tone lightens as my memories turn to my favorite show.

"Totally no judgment. That show was popular for what, seven years?"

"Yeah! Which is why a scene in the third season influenced my love for Paris."

"Really?"

"In the third season, when Emily is missing her friend Allison and looking for clues, she flashes back to the times they talked about taking a trip to Paris."

He nudges my shoulder and says, "Only *you* would fall in love with a city through a television show."

"Yes, only me. But that's why I want the Eiffel Tower to be the first place we explore."

They both nod in agreement.

Michael says, "Do you have any other plans in mind?"

"When Jenny and I got off the phone last night, I started researching. I found three other places nearby."

"How nearby are we talking?" Jenny asks.

"No more than a thirty-minute drive from our hotel."

"That's not bad! What are these 'other places'?"

"The Louvre, Rodin Museum, and Montmartre's Wall of Love. What do y'all think?"

"I love it, Luce."

"So, do I, Lucy," Michael agrees.

"The best part is, those sites have something for everyone. Jenny loves history and adventure, I have dreamed of seeing the Eiffel Tower in person for years, and Michael, you love art."

Jenny says, "I have a feeling you have more reasons for bringing those specific places up."

Michael says, "Are you holding out on us again, girl?"

"No, no. I just haven't gotten there yet."

"Well, get on with it, won't you?" Michael prompts me.

"I picked those as potential article topics." Suddenly my phone buzzes. "Y'all, it's my editor in chief, Ashley Wilson."

Jenny says, "Open it! Open it!"

Michael says, "Go on, girl."

I take a deep breath and silently read the email over.

Bonjour Ms. Berry,

Thank you for your kind email. I am doing well. I thought over your pitches. I love them. The company values hearing up-to-date research on the most common tourist attractions. I am hoping your voice gives travelers a fresh outlook on these well-known and beloved Paris places. Those places are in great proximity to your location. The Eiffel Tower is marvelous. You will love it! With that being said, those four places will be your topics moving forward. To plan your trip—if you have a tentative writing/visiting schedule, send it over, and we will discuss the schedules and deadlines later this week.

As you move into starting your first assignment with your assigned editor, I want to remind you of *Getaway Travel Magazine's* mottos.

We Stand For: Building writers up, not tearing them down. Our writers are beginners to experts in their field, but all have a passion to share their perspectives of the world. We are adventurous and nonjudgmental.

Our Team Goals: We aim to produce uplifting, creative, and unique conversational-style articles with a dash of research. We want to spark curiosity and lead readers to discover the world.

Our Mission is to create a safe space for travelers to hear from real-life people about out-of-this-world destinations and experiences.

Thanks,
Ashley Wilson
Head Editor in Chief
*Getaway Travel Magazine*

"Ah!" I squeal.

Jenny taps on the table and says, "What? What did she say?"

"She said, 'I love them.'"

Jenny gives me a high five. "That's our girl."

Michael pokes my side and says, "Get it, girl. I'm so excited. One question, how are you able to write about well-known places?"

I tell them about how my pieces can give a fresh outlook. I need to make a tentative writing schedule for Mrs. Wilson to look over.

Jenny says, "Maybe we should pay and head to your house?"

"If y'all want to come over, y'all are more than welcome to come to hang and plan some more."

"I'm down. I love planning trips," Jenny says. "Can I invite Aaron over? I know he would love to hear about Paris and finally meet Michael. Well, that is, if you are coming over." She raises her eyes at him as we stand by the table.

Aaron has been my best friend since kindergarten. It was always him, me, and Jenny, the original trio. Now, he and Jenny have been married for a year and a half, a total of eight-and-a-half years together. I envy the love they have for one another—supportive, precious, and committed to each other. I couldn't think of a better duo than them.

"Aaron is more than welcomed to join." I eye Michael. "Are you coming, boi?"

"I'm down. Let's hang out before we spend four weeks together. Shall we?"

Michael opens the door for Jenny and me. We walk out of the restaurant into a very bright, sunny afternoon in Athens, Alabama. I shield my eyes as I head to my blue Nissan Versa. "I'll see y'all at the house. Michael, stay close behind Jenny or me since you haven't been there yet." My engine rumbles as I crank my car.

Jenny says, "Just watch for blue, or call us." She closes her door while Michael shakes his head and smiles at us.

I'm ready to roll out as Niall Horan's "Heartbreak Weather" streams through the speakers.

# CHAPTER 2

# SO CLOSE

———

## AUGUST 17, 2021

I pull into my driveway, and there's that sudden wave of nostalgia again. I try to push the feelings out of my mind, but they are relentless, a constant movie reel interrupting my day.

David's face flashes in my mind with that boyish grin that used to drive me wild and his brown hair falling in his eyes. All I can picture is him falling in love with her and leaving me with that same endearing look he always gave me. The memories are too much. I almost tear up, but my thoughts are interrupted by a car horn. In my rearview mirror, I see Jenny and Michael are simultaneously honking.

I turn off my car and step out into the driveway. I gesture for both of them to come on in the house, fumbling with my keys. Car doors close.

"Luce," Jenny says. "Aaron can't make it."

"Oh, no. Overtime at work?" I finally get my hands to cooperate. We shuffle into my house.

"No. Aaron sent a text saying that David called him and sounded uneasy. Uneasy? I would like to punch him."

"Jenny, dear, no violence. Those two are still best friends, and we must learn to deal with it." Even though David cheated on me, I didn't want him to lose both his wife and his best friend. I couldn't stomach it, nor would I want to sink to his level of betrayal. Instead, I accepted the life change for the sake of my sanity.

She scoffs, "How are you so chill?"

"Because I have accepted it! Well, part of me has. The other part is as mad as you are."

"He passed up seeing me and you for David. Why?"

"No idea. You have your phone, not me." I try to lighten the mood.

"Right, right. I knew that." She quickly scrolls through her missed texts from Aaron. "Okay, he also said he knows I'll be mad, but David worried him. He adds, 'David is my buddy, and I know Lucy will understand. She understood from the get-go. Please, Jen, don't be mad at me. Tell Lucy I am sorry.'" She huffs and rolls her eyes. "That was like five texts in a row because I didn't answer. Should I reply?"

"Hm, yeah?" I raise my eyebrow at her and say, "Assure him we aren't too mad. Just bummed that we aren't hanging out with him."

"Michael, do you agree?" Jenny anxiously taps her foot.

"I do, even without ever meeting Aaron, that is. I've met David all of once, but I am the one who helped y'all decide on the divorce." Michael shrugs. "Just be honest with him. That's all you can do."

"All right." She types away, then announces, "I sent it."

"Good, now relax," I say. "We have more information to cover. Then we are relaxing for real before all the packing begins this week."

"Relaxing, you say?"

"I'm going to pour a glass of wine. Y'all want some?"

Michael says, "You had me at wine. What do you have?"

Jenny says, "I bet she has Roscato." She always pokes fun at me for my love of the sweet red wine.

I grin and say, "Maybe I do, maybe I don't."

I look through the wine glasses in the cabinet and smile. Unlike most people, Jenny knows me well, especially concerning wine. I settle on my graduation glass, which holds a special place in my heart. My cousin Meredith got it with my mom and picked out the saying etched on the glass, *She believed she could, so she did.*

"Which glasses would y'all like? A stand or just the glass part?" Between special events and holidays, my wine glass collection is shaping up.

Tapping her chin, Jenny says, "I want one with a stand. It's easier to hold. Don't need any mishaps."

Michael quickly agrees. "Same! No wine will be spilled today!"

I can't help but shake my head as I reach to the back of the counter for the Roscato. I pour each of us a glass.

"I knew it!" Jenny squeals.

I roll my eyes and hand their glasses to them. I cup my hands around my glass and take a long sip. Roscato may be a dessert wine, but it hits the spot every time. Smooth and sweet, my trademark.

"Yum," Michael murmurs as he takes a big sip.

"Is it good?" I poke his side.

"Ha, sorry, I haven't had Roscato before."

I put my hand to my chest. "I am honored that I get to show you this hidden gem. Best friends drink wine together—it is just a known fact!"

One night while Jenny and I were at Olive Garden, a waiter recommended we try a glass of Roscato. I was hesitant at first because, before then, I hadn't tried many alcoholic beverages. He told us that it was sweet red wine, not bitter or too strong. We agreed to one glass each, and I have loved it ever since.

"Is it now? Are you sure you haven't already had wine today?"

"Excuse you, sir! How dare you suggest that!"

"Have you?" He raises his eyebrows.

"No, this is my first glass." They both give me a look. "I promise. Goodness, you two!"

"Are you sure you're okay?" Jenny puts her face right in front of me and stares straight into my eyes.

"I'm fine. Do I still have flashbacks? Yes. Do I have dreams? Not anymore. Do I drink more wine now? Kinda. But, I am fine." I walk toward the living room. "Let's go sit down and talk."

I fall into my chair while Jenny and Michael sit on the couch adjacent to me.

"What else do we need to cover, Luce?" Jenny asks as she sits cross-legged, like an eager child waiting for a movie to start playing on the television.

"How much money we want to take, a packing list, and a tentative writing plan." I grab my silver laptop from the coffee table. "I'll start with Googling the ideal packing list."

I type in "How do you pack for a Paris trip" in the search bar. The first article result reads "Seventeen Top Paris Packing List Items for 2020 Plus What to Wear."

"Oh, I think I found something. Let me get my notebook so I can write these down." I hurry out of the room and to my writing area. My pink notebook sticks out from under some papers. I grab it and my Minnie Mouse pen and hurry back.

"Walking loud enough?" Michael teases as I plop down in my chair and huff.

"Yes. As a matter of fact, I am walking the right volume."

"Maybe no more wine?" He eyes my almost empty glass.

"I didn't even have that much, to begin with! Back to business. This 2020 article looks helpful."

"Lucy, darling, it is 2021." He smirks. I can tell they are both trying not to go into a laughing fit. It wasn't *that* funny.

"The article is literally from 2020, you guys."

"We are just joking with you, Luce," Jenny says.

"Yes, I know, I know. I am just a tad stressed. I had a flashback of David today before lunch and after." I sigh as I jot down some packing essentials.

Michael says, "Girl, why didn't you tell us?"

"Because I wanted to talk about *Paris*, not my *divorce*." I shrug. Michael and Jenny come and sit on the arms of my chair. "Y'all, really, I'm okay. I just want to focus on the trip, my writing, and my two best friends." They give me a hug. "Ah, Lucy sandwich much?"

"No, a *best friend* sandwich. We are bonding." Michael laughs in my ear.

Jenny says, "Yes, we are bonding, Lucy Lu." She hasn't called me Lucy Lu in ages. It feels like a breath of fresh air. Hopefully, a sign that my past isn't all that bad.

"Yeah, Lucy Lu, get with the bonding program."

"I'm trying, I'm trying."

"There's that laugh," Jenny says as they both squeeze me again.

I wiggle and twist in the middle of them. "Okay, okay, time to get this planning on a roll." I push out of the circle. "Maybe we should just sit on the floor with my laptop on the coffee table?"

"I like that idea," Jenny says and slides off the chair, beating Michael and me to the floor. "Probably way easier for us all to see the list." She sits crisscross as she waits for us.

"I guess that's settled." Michael joins Jenny on the floor. I plop on the floor.

"Welcome to the floor. How may we help you?" Jenny says.

"Yes, I would like to show y'all these essential packing items. Would y'all be interested in hearing more?" I ask in my best customer-service voice.

Michael points to the screen and says, "What is *that*?"

"The article says, 'The universal power adapter allows the user to charge their devices anywhere. Other destinations include London, Ireland, Europe, and over one hundred countries.' Hey, didn't you go to London two summers ago?"

"My parents took me for my college graduation trip last year."

"Okay, so do you still have an adapter, or should we order one?" While he thinks, I click on the Amazon link as a backup. Fingers crossed he has one.

"I've got it covered. My parents and I have two, so I can bring them."

"That's settled. Let me start a new page for our packing list. Hmm, do you happen to have jet lag relief?"

"Not sure. Go ahead and add it to your cart."

"All right, added. Moving on, the next item is a windproof travel umbrella. Oh goodness, that price is high! Please tell me you bought one back then?"

"Yes! We're good! I'll bring mine. Breathe, Lucy!"

"She doesn't know what breathing is," Jenny pipes up.

"I do too." I roll my eyes.

Michael says, "So you do, and we are glad."

Over the next hour, we compile a rough packing list. We have everything from new travel items to everyday self-care and medical items. It is better to be overprepared when we start packing than to run around our houses like chickens with their heads cut off. Traveling out of the country doesn't call for panic packing. We needed a game plan.

Michael breaks the silence and says, "What's next?"

I say, "Oh, we need to get tickets for the attractions as well."

Jenny says, "Hmm, uh, that's important. I'm guessing that's one of the things the magazine company doesn't include?" She gives me a puzzled look.

"One of the few, but we've got this." I fake crack my knuckles and get to work.

Twenty minutes later, we have a complete main attractions cost list for a one-day visit to each. Between tickets and a guided tour, the price for all four attractions isn't going to break the bank. Considering the Wall of Love is free, we are doing good. Our largest money chunk guarantees we get to explore the entire Eiffel Tower from top to bottom in one day. A dream come true. We plan to split the cost for each ticket total and budget extra for souvenirs and food.

I look over the list. "Considering the magazine pays for a chunk of the expenses, this isn't too bad."

Jenny says, "We are spacing those visits out, right?"

"Yes. Here's what my tentative schedule looks like now. Day one, we visit the Eiffel Tower for our tour, then the rest of that week is writing, editing, exploring, and research. Each week ends, and then a new place begins. Terrible or good?"

Michael says, "I think your plan gives us more time to chill. We can look up the shopping places, food, and normal sightseeing."

We scroll through the "Top Twenty Free Things to Do in Paris" article. I say, "Let's make a list of free places to go to while in Paris."

We go silent as I write down four interesting places with their descriptions and addresses on my paper. A good half hour later, I prop my notebook on my bent knees. I feel accomplished. We have packing essentials, attractions, and now free Paris sights.

We are ready for you, Paris.

Michael leans over and inspects the list. "I am really intrigued by that haunted cemetery."

I poke his side. "It would be a really good setting for a horror story or poem."

"Oh, yes, it would be. Maybe I'll do some writing, too. I want to publish some horror poems and short stories someday."

"Do you want to publish a collection of each or a combination?"

"I don't know yet. I like the combination part. Maybe I'll do short, long, and prose poems in one collection."

"Whatever makes your spooky heart happy, Sparks." I smile. "Jenny, do you see anything that sparks that history and adventure brain of yours?"

Jenny squeals. "Ah, the park has a rich history. I'm totally down for that one!"

"This trip is going to be epic! There really is something for all of us to enjoy. I can't wait to share it with y'all." I take a deep breath. The trip is coming together nicely.

"Does that mean we can relax now? You must be tired from staring at your computer all afternoon."

Michael checks his phone. "It is almost five. I don't need to be home anytime soon. We should relax some more. What do you say, girl? Want company for a little longer?"

I grin. "I always want y'all's company. We need food and a good movie. What do y'all think?"

"Pizza and wine always hits the spot." He raises his eyebrows.

Jenny looks at me and grins. "All right, Michael, you are my favorite. Lucy, he speaks our language."

"I always knew he would."

By six o'clock, we have pizza, Roscato red wine, and *Passport to Paris*, a major 2000s throwback playing on my TV. I am genuinely happy without David. Our marriage ended a year ago, and he just announced his engagement. I have every right to be happy, too. Not that I wasn't before the announcement, but I deserve to find love again. I deserve to find that special someone, just like he did. Except I will be doing it as a single woman, not a married woman. Maybe I am still bitter. In my defense, only a year has passed, and he stayed with her. What's a girl to do? Sit back and be rainbows and sunshine about the situation? If only that was how the last year of my life went, but it wasn't the way my story continued after him.

# CHAPTER 3

# LET'S JET!

———

## AUGUST 24, 2021

I'm ready to be a million miles away from him, the nightmares, and my past. He can't get me while I'm in another country... or can he?

I desperately try to push him out of my head and check last week's emails again.

Good Evening,

I hope this email finds you well. So close to Paris! I have that article schedule idea for you. Let me know if this is the type of layout the magazine is looking for. I look forward to hearing back from you and talking about the trip and articles.

Article Schedule:

- Email articles by deadlines!
- 4 weeks / 4 articles
- Eiffel Tower: start article on August 26— Due September 5.

- Writing / Research / Exploring
- The Louvre: start article on September 2—
  Due September 12.
- Writing / Research / Exploring
- Rodin Museum: start article on September 9—
  Due September 19.
- Writing / Research / Exploring
- Wall of Love: start article on September 16—
  Due September 26.

Leave Paris September 21.
Thanks,
Lucy Berry


Hello Ms. Berry,

I am doing well, and I hope the same for you. I am very impressed with your article schedule layout. It works well because it keeps you writing. Just remember to be mindful of editing. Although you will be emailing it to an editor, helping with edits is a great thing for a writer and editor relationship. I will give you your editor's information now, so you can have that before you jet off to Paris next week.

Judith Garcia
Editor in Chief
*Getaway Travel Magazine*
jgarcia@getawaytravelmag.com

Thanks,

Ashley Wilson
Head Editor in Chief
*Getaway Travel Magazine*

"Oh, Lucy, my sweetheart. I love you," he says. He reaches out to me. His hands are rough, and pencil smudges line his thumbs. Another long day of editing someone else's book and sending it to publishing.

I feel dizzy. I back away from David as his fingers inch closer to my shoulders. "But do you? Do you really love me?"

"I really do, honest. I have for nearly ten years."

"I don't believe you." I place my palms on the wall. "This isn't real. You aren't real. We aren't together."

"Sweetheart, I swear you are the only woman for me." He almost grabs my wrist, but I shift away, almost losing my balance.

"I—I don't love you. I don't love you. Leave me alone, David. Get out of my sight. Go away. You are a liar and a cheater."

He pins my hands above my head and pushes me against the wall with his body. He looks into my eyes and says, "You love me. I love you. You can't run away from me." I struggle and kick my feet. He smashes me into the wall harder. "You can't hide from me."

I close my eyes and scream.

Beams of sweat sting my eyes and my heart races. He can't be here. The locks were changed ages ago. His keys won't work anymore. My parents have an extra key, everything is fine.

They're at their house. David's somewhere else. My house is safe, secure, and David free. Rubbing my eyes, I check my phone and groan. It's only five o'clock. Apparently, nightmares have no mercy for the weak. After slowing my breathing and sending a text to the group, my body starts to relax.

Me: Good morning! It's Paris day. Wake up. Let's meet at my house at 6:50.

Jenny: I'm up! Goodness, it is too early for this.

Michael: I am barely awake. Wait, where is your house again, Lucy?

Jenny: Ugh. It's five in the morning. Why?

Me: Early bird gets the worm.

Michael: I am in Huntsville. Should I meet y'all there instead, otherwise I would be backtracking?

Me: Oops, boi, you are right. Meet us at the airport at eight. Speaking of backtracking, Jenny, your house is closer to the airport than mine. I can just pick you up around 7:10.

Jenny: I love that idea. Look whose brain is going ninety miles per hour at five a.m.

Michael: Only Lucy. See y'all at eight.

Jenny: So true. See you then.

Me: Thanks y'all! No one fall back asleep!

Jenny: Yes, MOM!

Michael: Okay, MOM!

Me: Yes, I know I'm older. Ha! Very funny!


The nightmare fades to the back of my mind. I slowly start to breathe as I head for the front door. Soon I will be on a different continent from my cheating ex-husband. For the next four weeks, I will be indulging my time and energy in enjoying the French culture with my two best friends. What could go wrong?

Twenty minutes later, I pull into Aaron and Jenny's driveway. I sit in my car for a minute and admire their cute, white-paneled house. Her front door is green, like mine. We really are best friends. Our styles are easy to mix and match yet unique to our personalities. The light breeze gently pushes the wooden porch swing. Back and forth, back and forth, my eyes follow the chains.

My tennis shoes hit the pavement. Jenny waves wildly from the porch as the front door creaks on its hinges. I yell, "I'm coming! I'm coming!"

"Lucy, hurry up." She claps her hands. "Get a move on."

"Jenny, dear, slow down. We have time." I huff as I walk up the steps.

She tilts her head. "Are you okay?"

I can tell my mood is concerning her, but I don't feel like sharing my thoughts. I want to be happy and fly to *Paris*. I shrug. "I'm tired," I half-lie. "I'll probably sleep on the flight."

"Uh-huh. I don't buy it for a second. I'll let you have a free pass since we are jetting off to Paris! Man, I've always wanted to say that."

"Of course."

We walk into their house. Her luggage is neatly lined against the wall. Her keys gleam in the ceramic bowl on the table. A vase of fresh flowers sits beside it. "Did Aaron get you flowers?" I sniff the lilacs, a beautiful purple and pink bouquet. "I love them."

"Yeah, he got them for me the other day." She smiles. "He's around here somewhere."

"Oh, Aaron, are you going to come to say bye to us?"

Aaron pops his head around the corner. He runs his fingers through his shaggy brown hair as he walks over and kisses Jenny on the cheek.

"Y'all are even cute in the morning. How?"

Aaron's blue eyes gleam, and he says, "I'm not much of a morning person, but for her, I can be."

I gag. "Too much cuteness."

"Oh, no. You called me in here. You are getting all the cuteness." He pulls Jenny from behind and wraps his arms around her waist. Laying his head on her shoulder, he grins and adds, "You know you love us." He kisses Jenny on the forehead.

"Okay, okay, don't make me a third wheel." I check my phone. "We've got to get going."

Jenny says, "What, already?"

"Yes, already."

Aaron pulls Jenny closer. "No, y'all are staying. I will not let y'all leave for four weeks." He shakes his head. "Nope, not happening."

My phone rings. It's Michael. I answer and say, "Good morning, boi."

He starts rambling. "Have y'all left Athens yet? What time should I leave? Where are we meeting? The gate, right?"

"Michael, slow down. Are you okay?"

"You know, just a little panic in the morning. No big deal. How are you?"

"I know the feeling, but I'm good. I'm with Jenny and Aaron right now."

Jenny says, "Are you at least ready for Paris?"

Michael admits, "I'm going to miss my cats and parents, but I need a getaway from Alabama. Loads of writing inspiration on the horizon, gals."

"That's the spirit!" Jenny and I say together.

Aaron says, "Y'all must be best friends."

Michael says, "Hey, dude, I think that makes us best friends, too."

"Dude, it does!"

I shake my head and say, "We've got to go, y'all."

Aaron leans toward my phone. "We can continue this later, Michael. In the meantime, keep our girls safe."

My heart melts. He is still one of my favorite guys.

Jenny and I hug Aaron. He says, "I'm counting on you, Michael."

Michael says, "You have my word."

To Michael, I say, "We'll call you from the road in about fifteen minutes. Love you, Sparks."

Michael says, "Talk to y'all soon. Bye!"

"Bye!"

The call ends, and Aaron squeezes us tighter. He says, "One. More. Minute."

I manage to pry myself from his arms. "Aaron, we love you, and we'll see you in four weeks." I grab Jenny's hand and tug her to me. "You're mine now."

Aaron pouts while he loads Jenny's suitcase. She smiles at him, and his face softens. He gives us one more hug and quickly runs to the porch to wave at us.

I turn to Jenny. "Let's go!"

# CHAPTER 4

# BONJOUR, FRIENDS

———

## AUGUST 24–25, 2021

We board the plane and walk down the narrow aisles. "We're in the middle rows. Jenny and I are in one. Michael, you are behind us."

Michael looks stylish yet comfy in his blue-and-white-striped sweater. Rolling up his sleeves, he slides into his row and beams. "Oh, I got a window seat."

I slide next to the window. "Well, for *this* part of the flight, yes."

"I guess it won't be so bad to not have a window seat the next time. Since the next flight isn't over Paris."

Jenny says, "Oh, I hope that's the case." Her Harry Styles T-Shirt wrinkles as she bumps my shoulder.

"It definitely is. I know how to plan," I exclaim. We each get a window seat during one or more of the flights." I smooth down my Charlie Puth T-Shirt, feeling accomplished.

Jenny wiggled her eyebrows. "You know us so well, Lucy Lu."

"Nah, I just know if I'm not asleep, I'll be looking out the window."

Michael leans up as the seatbelt sign flashes and says, "Are you going to sleep?"

"I'll see y'all in Atlanta."


David stares at me. A mischievous smile plays across his lips. He says, "You're back. How fun."

I nervously twist my ring and say, "I don't love you. I don't want to be here." I have my hands behind my back as I inch slowly away from him toward the front door.

He quickly catches up to me. I grab the doorknob. He grips my other hand and yanks me into the living room. I stumble, and my fingers graze the top of a picture frame. Holding my hand to my face, I stare at my simple diamond-cut ring with a plain band behind it. My wedding ring. It can't be.

I hold up my hand. "What is this?"

He grins and holds up his left hand. "We're married, sugar. I'm all yours."

I cradle my hand and shrink against the wall. "I'm not your anything. Your hers." I feel small.

"No, I'm yours. Forever and always until death do us part, sweetheart."

"Uh—uh, sir, you two deserve each other. Stay away from me," I scream. He reaches for me, and I back away.

"It's our anniversary week, sugar. We have to celebrate."

"Over my dead body!" I leap up and sprint toward the door.

He grabs my wrist and throws me on the couch. He pins me by both wrists and straddles my waist. Leaning down, he whispers, "I'll never go away. I love you."

"Lucy, Lucy, hey Lucy! Wake up!" I open one eye, and Jenny is shaking my shoulder. She says, "We just landed in Atlanta."

"Ugh!" I groan.

"Oh, don't give me that," she teases. "We are one stop closer to sweet *Paris*."

Michael leans into mine and Jenny's aisle and gives me a big smile. He cheers, "Yeah, one stop down."

I try to hide my pain with a smile. "I'm just tired, okay?"

Jenny rolls her eyes. "You'll perk up once you have some food in you."

"Did you say food?"

"*There's* the Lucy we love."

"Hm, duh! Now, what about the food?" We walk down the ramp into the busy airport.

"While you were sleeping, I used the plane Wi-Fi to Google what we can buy to eat at this airport," Jenny says. "Michael and I decided that Ginger's Burgers sounded yummy!"

Michael points to a retro-style tiny burger joint. "I found it."

I can smell the burgers on the grill, sizzling behind the open counter. My stomach growls as we walk into the restaurant. A waitress guides us to a booth close to the counter. I slide in next to Michael, and Jenny sits across from me.

I say, "Y'all, I need to confess something." I prop my chin on my hands. "I had another nightmare about David."

Jenny arches her eyebrows and calmly says, "Wait, another?"

"Yeah, I had two today. One woke me up at five o'clock, sorry. Then, the one on the plane." I slowly rub my arms as chill bumps pop up. "They were both so scary and felt real."

Michael says, "Scary?"

"It was like the night of mine and David's fight, but much more intense."

"Like your brain ramped up the pain?"

"Exactly. In both, David thought we were still married. He was aggressive. But in the second one, we both had our wedding rings on." Their jaws drop. "He said it was our anniversary week, and we had to celebrate." They continue to stare with their jaws open. "He kept insisting that I was the only woman for him. He pinned me against the walls and the couch." Anger swells in my chest. "It was like that night all over again, but much, much worse."

Jenny snorts. "I have no words, other than that jerk!"

Michael fumes. "I second that."

I move my fries around my plate. "I don't know how to feel other than angry that he's in my head."

"Feel anything you want to, girl. Let it all out."

Jenny says, "You have to get it out somehow. How does him pinning you down make you feel?"

"Angry."

"What are you going to channel that into, Lucy Lu?"

"I'm going to fight him off." I hit my fist on the table, "No more David nightmares."

"If you can fight off those nightmares, you can do anything, gal." We fist bump as we get ready to leave the restaurant. Our flight is still three hours out.

"I could fight off a bear if I wanted to. I was married to one, after all!"

Michael says, "Dang, girl."

"Well, it is the honest truth." I shrug. "He's out of my life. Now, to get him out of my head. Surely, it can't be *that* hard. The nightmares stopped before. They'll stop again."


"Lucy, you dozed off," Jenny says and pokes my shoulder. "We're flying over Paris. Look out the window."

I burst forward in my seat. I yell, "Wait, we are over Paris right now?"

"Yes!" Jenny squeals. People stare at us.

Michael cups his ears and says, "Squeal often?"

"*Very* often, actually. It's a normal thing."

I grin. "Welcome to *my* world, Sparks."

A tiny glimpse of Paris resides beneath us. The Eiffel Tower looms over the magnificent buildings. Sun rays beam off every structure with elegant grace and beauty, casting a heavenly glow over the beautiful city.

"Soon, we will be at the ORY airport. Paris is calling, and I am picking up," I say. "Hi, Paris, yes, I would *love* to stay for four weeks!"

The intercom crackling snaps me back to reality as the pilot's voice echoes through the aircraft.

"Okay, folks, welcome to Paris, France."

# CHAPTER 5

# PARIS AWAITS

---

## AUGUST 25, 2021

After settling into our hotel room on the third floor, we hurry back outside and wait for a taxi. The Cler Hotel sits on a busy street about a mile from the Eiffel Tower. Colorful fruits line the stand attached to the elegant white building framed with tall windows. A few minutes later, we flag down a small taxi driving up the narrow road. Our driver says, "First time in Paris?"

I beam. "Yes, sir. We landed a little after eleven this morning."

The driver turns onto a small busy street, *Avenue de la Motte-Picquet,* and Michael asks, "Do you have any suggestions for us?"

The cheery driver says, "In about four minutes, we will be crossing the Seine River, where boats run all throughout the day until seven. The Seine goes by the Eiffel Tower, Cathedral Notre-Dame de Paris, Louvre Museum, which are some of the most notable."

"Oh!" I exclaim. "I read about the Seine River Cruise. It sounds lovely!"

"It really is. I would say the best time to hop on is midafternoon or the last boat that goes out because the city lit up is incredible."

"The Eiffel Tower's lights are on, right?" Jenny says.

"Yes, they are! With the background of the night sky, you are in for a treat. Tourists and locals alike love sitting in the grass in front of the Eiffel Tower as the sun sets behind it." He turns left onto *Rue du Petit Pont*. "But, for now, we are almost at Shakespeare and Company, famous for its collection of classic used books."

I look from Jenny to Michael. I gush, "See, the perfect first place to visit."

The street is busy with people walking up and down the sidewalk. The driver leans out the window and hollers, "Enjoy your trip."

Shakespeare and Company's green window frames and yellow sign immediately jump out at me. Books fill the windows, and a picture of Shakespeare is mounted above the door. Writers come from all over to draw inspiration from the hundreds of books.

"I can't believe we are actually in Paris," I squeal as we enter the bookstore.

As we walk up the red wooden staircase, different-color book spines fill my vision. The smell of old books calms me. Rolling ladders sit at the end of each towering shelf. Books are stacked to the ceiling like we are in the Beast's library or browsing Rapunzel's collection. I am in my happy place.

A white spine with blue lettering catches my eye. The title and author immediately throw me back to my engagement with David and the movie we went to see that night. A date full of surprises. How could I have known it wouldn't last?

I barely hear Jenny's voice. It comes through low, almost a whisper. "Lucy, what did you find?" She leans a little closer to look at the cover. "*Everything, Everything* by Nicola Yoon. Haven't you read this one?"

"I—I have," I stammer.

"I remember you lending me your copy."

"I did," I shakily confirm.

Michael gently observes, "Are you okay, girl?"

"Engagement. Surprise date. Movie. David—" My chest rises and falls. I can't breathe. The room is spinning. My heart is racing.

Jenny says, "Oh, chickadee. You are miles, miles, and *miles* away from that two-faced jerk. Don't let him affect one of your favorite books and movies."

Michael thumbs through the shelf in front of us. "Look around you, girl. You are in a bookshop in the middle of *Paris*."

I clutch the book to my chest and take a deep breath. "I know y'all are right, but everything feels so heavy. He won't leave me alone. Am I allowed to be happy?"

Jenny says, "Yes, you are allowed to be whatever you want to be. He can't limit you here or anywhere." She gently takes the book from me and places it back on the shelf.

"Can I really, truly, move on? Be honest."

"It's possible. Honest," she assures me. "Yes, it'll take time, and I'm going to try not to push you."

"No pushing at all?"

"Okay, maybe a little," she admits.

I shake my head. "Michael, are you going to be her accomplice?"

"Only for your own good." Michael shrugs. "A little push never hurt anyone."

"A poke here and there," Jenny teases. "We've got your back, Lucy Lu."

"Well, okay, my loyal pokers" I giggle. "How do you plan to shift my mood?"

"Close your eyes."

"Okay." I tightly close my eyes and wait. They each grab my hand and spin it in a circular motion. "Can I open my eyes?"

"Yes."

My hand is pointing at a yellow spine. I run my fingers over the cover of *Perks of Being A Wallflower* by Stephen Chbosky. "I've been wanting to read this book."

Jenny says, "It's fate."

"Maybe y'all are my good luck charms."

Michael says, "I think you are cuckoo, but I love you."

"We are all a bit crazy about books."

"Books fuel this trio."

Jenny hollers, "Even me!"

"Books bring people together."

I wipe a tear from my eye. "We are all too sappy for our own good."

Michael wags his finger and says, "We don't need any tears, other than happy tears, missy."

"There will definitely be happy tears when we see the Eiffel Tower tonight," I cheer as my mood shifts back to normal.

"I can see it now." Jenny waves her hands across the air. "As soon as Lucy gets a glimpse, tears will start streaming down her face."

"You're probably right."

"I think we all will," Michael agrees.

"I know a way to make this day even sappier," I suggest.

"How?"

"We each buy a book. A token from the heart of Paris." I pull my choice to my chest. "Let's end this bookshop trip on a high note. Does anything catch your eye?" We browse the many shelves. I wonder if anyone has even tried to count them. My head hurts thinking about it.

"Not really." Jenny frowns. "I haven't felt a pull to one yet."

Michael says, "I spotted a poetry book I like. It isn't horror, but it is by someone both you and I like, Lucy." He winks at me, and I wink back.

Jenny waves her hand in front of us. "Hello, fill me in, y'all."

"Oh, right. We have our very own poetry virgin."

Michael gasped, "Lucy, that's something I would say, not you."

"It was a moment I couldn't pass up."

Michael shakes his head. "Anyway, I found *The Sun and Her Flowers* by Rupi Kaur." He plucks out a tiny book from the top shelf. The cover is creamy-white with yellow flowers.

I ask Jenny, "Do you want to read some of her poetry when we get back to Athens?"

"What's her poetry like?"

Michael says, "She writes freestyle poetry, which is why Lucy and I love her poems."

"Freestyle?"

"Little to no rhyming."

"No rhyming? Okay, I'll give it a try."

I pump my fist in the air and say, "We will make you into a poetry reader!"

"And the *Breakfast Club* has made it to France!" Jenny laughs.


After an early dinner at Paris' Pizzeria, we looked up where to buy macarons. The sugary, mouthwatering treats were in a castle-like building with pale-green and gold accents. Even the name sounded medieval—Ladurée. Little did we know there would be tons of flavors. From dark to bright tones, this shop had it all. After selecting, bagging, and purchasing our first Paris treats, we walked to the Eiffel Tower lawn with the sun streaming down on us.

I pat the blanket we bought while exploring and say, "Where should we sit?"

Jenny points to the lawn's middle path closer to the Eiffel Tower. A better view than I expected for our first night. We walk around at least ten lovey-dovey couples staring at only their partner. Deeply in love. Aren't they lucky? My stomach drops as we plop down on our blanket and unwrap our macarons.

Jenny murmurs, "Mmmm. So good."

I nudge her shoulder. "Is it good, Jen?"

She nods as she takes another bite.

Michael gives me a side-eye and says, "Oh, yes." He holds his macaron out like a food show host. "Yes, this is a fine piece of cookie. You see, here," he continues, "the filling is also coffee flavored like the shells, but it is buttercream. How incredible is that?"

Jenny finishes her first macaron and jumps right in with Michael's monologue. "Yes, Mr. Sparks, you have a great point." She holds up her lemon-flavored cookie. "These little gems are famous for their sugary taste and colorful shells. Wouldn't you agree?"

"Mrs. Morgan, you are so correct in your review. French culture has really outdone itself this time."

"Incredibly so." She holds her hand up to me like a microphone. "Miss, Miss, how do these little delights make you feel?"

I hold up my pink one and say, "Thank you for asking, ma'am. Yes, I love these little gems. They are light, delicious, and elegant. An essential part of the Paris experience."

Jenny smiles and acts like she's directing. "And... *scene.*"

Michael says, "Why are we cutting?"

Jenny says, "Look around. The sun is close to setting."

"Oh, oh!" he exclaims.

I finished my second macaron and reclined back. A blue tone highlights the sky, making the tower glow brighter. The lights twinkle from top to bottom, casting a bright glow on the lawn.

I muse, "This view is more than I imagined."

"I agree. This is a magical moment."

"Like a love potion is being cast all over the city." I glance at all the couples again. This city is full of beautiful love stories, both romance and friendship.

Jenny says, "Do you think you could fall in love here, Lucy?"

"All I know is, I don't ever want to lose myself to love again. At this moment, I would rather love myself than jump into a relationship." My mind drifts off as I think about the possibilities of falling in love again. Can I give my full heart to someone after such a devastating heartbreak? Can I find love after David? Am I ready to take that leap?

# CHAPTER 6

# EIFFEL TOWER

---

## AUGUST 26, 2021

The Eiffel Tower gleams in the morning sun. Soft shadows cover the sidewalk. The light breeze ruffles my hair. Our tour starts in thirty minutes. The area is packed from gate to gate. After a few minutes, we are guided into the elevator. We ascend through the tower's inner parts. The elevator comes to an immediate stop. The subway-style doors slide open on the first floor. I say, "Whoa!"

Michael grabs our hands and zooms all the way to the railing. I put my hands on my hips and breathed deeply. Michael is smiling, proud of himself. I roll my eyes and tug them toward the tour guide, a petite woman in business casual.

Our tour guide finally gets everyone's attention and says, "Welcome to the Eiffel Tower Tour. I'm Sally Andrews." She walks a few paces toward the transparent glass floor. "The Eiffel Tower was completed once and for all, on March 31, 1889, and was the world's tallest structure for forty-one years. Raise your hand if Paris was on your bucket list?"

I raise my hand. I have dreamed of visiting Paris and the Eiffel Tower for as long as I can remember. The city's magic, wonder, and endless possibilities always drew me in. At twenty-six years old, I am finally on my dream trip.

"Ah. We have some dreamers today. Excellent."

A girl says, "The Eiffel Tower was a part of the French Revolution, right?"

"Yes, ma'am. Gustave Eiffel built the Eiffel Tower for the 1889 *Exposition Universelle*, an event celebrating the one-hundred-year anniversary of the French Revolution. This year the tower is celebrating one hundred thirty-two years since completion. Remarkable, isn't it?"

I raise my hand and confidently say, "Is it true that the Eiffel Tower was temporary at one time?"

She sadly says, "Yes, ma'am, at one time, the Eiffel Tower wasn't loved by everyone."

"It's known around the world now. What changed?"

"Most don't know that the tower was originally a proposal for the competition in the Exposition Universelle event where the competitors had to build an iron tower with a square base one hundred twenty-five meters wide and three hundred meters high. After much consideration and criticism, Gustave's idea was chosen. To think we almost didn't have an Eiffel Tower. Now that's something to think about, people." She waves her hand. "Come along this way. Our journey continues to the second floor."

Seconds later, we are ascending through the tower's inner parts once again. Sally announces, "Welcome to the heart of the tower." I lean against the elevator's glass-paneled walls and gasp at the unique iron craftsmanship throughout the structure.

The elevator dings and the doors slide open on the second floor. A cool breeze brushes against my cheeks. Jenny says, "Wow, Lucy, this is incredible."

I gasp at the breathtaking view and say, "I can't believe we are actually here."

Michael says, "I am blown away, gals."

Sally says, "On this floor, some of Paris's most famous monuments are visible: the Louvre, Grand Palais, the bends in the Seine, Montmartre, Invalides, Notre-Dame, and many more."

We walk over to the railing, and Sally points out the Louvre, which is nestled on the right side of the Seine River. Even from a distance, the building is beautiful. The glass pyramid's peak gleams in the soft sunlight, a tiny spec of Paris's greatest tourist attractions rising above the many artist hotspots. Next, she points to the water and says, "The Seine River is separated into the Left and Right Bank. But one of the neatest facts, perhaps, may be that the Left Bank holds everything an artistic person could dream of, from museums and monuments to cafés and gardens. Artists, writers, and philosophers from the early eras of Paris's art community history found their inspiration there, as well."

Jenny nudges my shoulder and says, "No wonder you picked the places you did. Aren't they almost all on the Left Bank?"

"I think so," I say hesitantly, "since they are all art related."

She props her hands on the railing and looks out at the cityscape. "Why don't you ask?"

I speak up and ask, "The Wall of Love is on the Left Bank, correct?

"That's a great question. Montmartre is on the Left Bank, and a pinnacle location for love in the neighborhood of Montmartre, as it is *The Wall of Love*," she laughs. "The neighborhood itself was vibrant with art history and whimsical charm even before the Revolution. The neighborhood was the hub for so many artists." I drift off as Sally talks about the famous French monuments around the city while pointing out the various parts of the landscape. I lean on the railing, gazing at the horizon, lost in thought.

Jenny bumps my hip, bringing me down to Earth or as close as the Eiffel Tower can let me. I dial back into Sally's monologue, just in time. "Ladies and Gents now is the big moment in the tour. We are on our way to the top of this beautiful structure."

Jenny hugs me from behind, lays her chin on my shoulder, and whispers in my ear, "All your dreams are going to come true, chickadee. This is just the first step!" She squeezes me.

"Welcome to the summit, ladies and gents. The top is home to Gustave Eiffel's office, panoramic maps, the 1889 summit model, and the champagne bar." She smiles. "This is where I leave you. Explore, grab something from the bar, but keep in mind you only have about a half-hour left in the tour tickets. Enjoy!"

I call out to Sally, "Wait, after the tickets are up, we can still explore the second and first floor, right?"

"Great question. Yes, but go down and buy general admission tickets from the booth. They are eleven euros each for the first and second-floor access. Then seventeen euros to include the summit. But note this, if you leave today, no re-entry until it opens tomorrow. A good tip, I might add."

"Oh. Thank you."

"No problem. It's my job. Enjoy the sights."

I turn to Jenny and Michael and say, "Champagne is a must, and I want to at least peek at Eiffel's office. Then, we can just come back another day and spend as long as we want."

Michael grins and says, "I'm always down to drink some champagne."

"Oh, we know you are."

"A man and his champagne, there's nothing better."

I squint at the rather small menu. "Mr. Sparks, which would you recommend, the white or rosé?"

"Definitely white for Jenny and me, but for you, my dear, a rosé."

Jenny says, "Now, I am all for white wine, but champagne? Why did you choose that for me?"

"I just get that vibe from you." Michael orders our drinks from the young-looking bartender. "I'll need two glasses of white champagne and one rosé champagne, kind sir."

His nametag gleams in the sun: Eric. He says, "Coming right up, sir."

Michael nudges my arm. "He's nice-looking, isn't he, Lucy?"

I drag them down the bar while Eric fills our glasses. "I will not hook up with a guy while we are on this trip!"

Jenny whines, "Ugh, why not? He's really cute."

"Yeah, Lucy, he's a cutie," Michael points out. "What's wrong with a little *fling* in Paris?"

"That right *there*."

"What right there?"

"You said, 'a little fling in Paris.'" I put air quotes around his phrase.

"So?"

"So? Seriously, you have to ask for my reason?" I angrily tap my foot.

"What's your reason?" Jenny tries to carefully slice through the tension.

"If you must know, I don't want a little fling." I pause to gather my thoughts. "Just because I got divorced, it doesn't mean I want to have a fling with just anyone. I still believe in love, soul mates, and marriage." I glance back at Eric, who waves us back over.

Michael scolds, "This conversation isn't over."

I dismiss his harsh tone with my hand and turn to Eric. "How much?"

"Forty-three euros." He smiles.

Our first full day flies by, and I am exhausted. Worn out from head to toe. From having a fabulous Eiffel Tower tour to walking around Paris, I am over the moon about today, as if I am coming home from a first date. The only thing missing is confidence in myself and my writing. I am stuck between being excited and concerned about writing my first article. At least I am writing about the Eiffel Tower, a way to ease myself into my new position.

Jenny and I are lying on our bed chatting and laughing as I try not to worry. Michael walks out of the bathroom, rubbing a towel over his dripping hair. His plaid pajama pants loosely rest on his hips, with his tank top meeting at his waistline. He catches my eye and smirks. Throwing the towel on the floor, he puts his hands on his hips and struts in front of us.

Jenny starts clapping and wooing. "Yes, work that catwalk, Mr. Sparks!"

He flashes us a winning smile. "And that's how Lucy is going to win over one of these fine-looking French men."

My jaw drops in shock. I shout, "No, Lucy, is not!"

"Yes, she most certainly is," he insists.

"No, I'm not." I cross my arms and scrunch up my nose. "I want a real connection, not a rebound."

"But, it'll be fun," he whines like a little boy.

"Pouting doesn't suit you."

Jenny says, "Come on, Lucy Lu, lighten up."

"Lighten up! Lighten up!" My eyes narrow at them. "I hate to state the obvious, but I will. I am on this trip for writing and my career. Quite frankly, I am glad to not be interested in anyone." I march over to the bathroom door and cup my hand around the handle. "I am a newly divorced woman who has only ever been with one man. He was my first and only love. It is harder for me than it seems. I am not, will not be, looking for someone new while in Paris. End of story."

I slam the bathroom door behind me, almost a little too hard for the small frame to handle. The door squeezes as it settles into place. I sink to the floor. Even in Paris, worlds away from all my problems, everything manages to pollute my thoughts and destroy my happiness. I can't let my problems destroy me.

I have to stand up for myself more often. I hate doing what I just did, but I had to. I just had to say it, or the conversation would have gone on forever and ever. I really didn't want four more weeks of focusing on getting me a casual fling with a cute French man. I will pass on that adventure.

I put my head in my hands and am trying to breathe deeply when I hear a knock on the door.

Michael's voice cracks, "Lucy, I'm sorry for pushing you. I didn't mean to, really. I got carried away."

I don't say anything.

"Am I going to have to sing to you?"

I smile.

"You don't have to come out because I know you probably want to shower and go to sleep, but I still want to know you are okay. We can't go to sleep angry."

I silently agree.

"I know you're mad. I know you may be sad. I know I can be a jerk, but I'm really sorry." He sings, "I love you to the moon and back more than he ever could. I'll be here until the end of time. It is you and me, my girl. You and me. So please say you at least hear me."

Silence. I am Elsa and he is Anna. I don't want to give in to him.

"You're my girl. My favorite person to bug and poke. You make me strong and whole. My best friend forever. Please say you'll forgive me."

I stare at the floor.

"I am so sorry, my dear Lucy. Sweet, sweet Lucy, you deserve the world. You deserve these adventures. I'll do better. Say you'll forgive me and tell me goodnight. Tell me we will be okay, and you hear my pleas."

I softly say, through the thin door, "I hear you. Go to sleep. I'm getting in the shower. Goodnight."

"Goodnight. Tomorrow will be better. I promise."

I smile and push myself off the marble floor.

# CHAPTER 7

# A VIEW FROM THE TOP

---

## AUGUST 28, 2021

Our room is quiet. It's only a few minutes after midnight, and I am the last one awake. The Eiffel Tower's twinkling lights float in the back of my mind like paper lanterns in the night sky. Dancing behind my heavy eyelids, the lights give me hope. Hope that he will leave my head, heart, and dream world. My body relaxes as I fluff my pillow. Sleep is coming. Finally, a peaceful night's rest is ahead.

"Lucy, why are you screaming?" I hear a voice in the distance. I can't see them. "Open your eyes. Are you okay?"

I groan and say, "Why are you shaking me?" I remove Jenny's hands from my shoulders.

Jenny says, "Your screaming woke us up. Plus, you kicked me." She rubs her knee.

I blush. "Sorry, another nightmare, but it had an upside, at least."

Michael says, "How can a nightmare have an upside?" He sits on the end of the bed staring at me.

"My monster ex-husband actually made a good point."
They both stare at me. "Wait, I'm not crazy."

"We didn't say you were, but him giving advice is crazy."
Jenny arches her eyebrows. "Don't you think?"

"Crazy, yes, but hear me out. Please." I poke my lip out.

They shrug their shoulders. Michael whispers something in Jenny's ear while glancing at me. I patiently wait for their verdict.

"Okay, what did the jerk say?" Michael hisses. "Uhm, I mean, what did he say?"

I roll my eyes and say, "He told me that holding on to him or letting him ruin my mind is keeping me locked in the past. He emphasized that it was time to escape."

"Ugh, why'd he have to go and make a good point?"

"He's still a jerk, though," Jenny scoffs.

"Jenny!" I gasp.

"What? Michael said it first." She crosses her arms. "We're the ones who love you. David's such a has-been."

I look to Michael for help. His eyes shift between Jenny and me. He slowly pats her shoulder and my foot. He explains, "Yes, I said David was a jerk, first, but I kind of see Lucy's point. She may have screamed, but when she woke up, she decided that she wasn't going to let him win. Rather, she took the high road. He may be a jerk, but," he holds his finger up, "in the end, healing has to happen, right?"

I suggest, "Maybe, I am finally starting to heal. Don't you want that, Jen?"

"Yes, of course, I do. I just don't like him messing with your thoughts. I believe you can come to healing on your own, without his nightmare insight." After a minute, she adds, "What if the terrible nightmares keep happening. What do you do then?"

"Aren't you the one who always says we'll cross that bridge when we come to it?"

"I am."

"So, we will do that. Let's be hopeful and face the other stuff when and if it arises."

Before she can agree, I pull them into a tight hug.

Michael says, "I love you both. I am so glad to be here. I am so sorry, Lucy, for being pushy yesterday. I shouldn't have assumed. That's so not like me."

I bury my face in his shoulder. "I forgive you. I can't really stay mad at you." I push away from them. "We may fight, but I know you'll always have my back."

"Always."

Jenny says, "Forever and always."


After an odd morning, I want to bring the focus back to my writing. Hopefully, I can. Only time will tell. For now, we are walking to the Eiffel Tower to start our fourth day in Paris, so I can immerse myself in my article topic. I tried researching books yesterday at the American Library, but everything was a bust. I couldn't match up my vision with the information I was reading. I went back to the drawing board. If my helpful nightmare taught me anything, it is to keep pushing forward. I'm not giving up on myself or my writing.

I look up the tower's iron structure and say, "Straight to the top?" They nod. We pack onto the small glass-panel elevator and zoom to the top. Sunlight blinds me as the doors slide open, and we shuffle out.

We lean on the Eiffel Tower's railing that overlooks the entire city. Jenny blushes as I barely hear her Harry Styles ringtone. A few seconds later, Aaron pops up on the screen. He is running his fingers through his messy hair.

Jenny says, "Aaron, can you see and hear us?"

"Yeah, yeah, I can see and hear you just fine." He smiles. "It is so good to see y'all. Are y'all at the Eiffel Tower now?"

Jenny moves her phone around to show Aaron the tower and the view. "We are on the top floor. Look at this view."

She is so excited to be talking to her favorite guy, even from miles away. Sometimes I envy how their marriage turned out amazing, and mine crashed and burned. Then I remember that Aaron is very different from David in every possible way. How they go about going to a bar with the guys speaks volumes to their character and commitment goals. One understands commitment while the other pushes the limits to the extreme. Honestly, I hope David learns from Aaron, not for me, but for his new bride-to-be, Alice.

"Earth to Lucy! Hey!" Aaron's voice brings me back to reality. "You okay over there?"

"Are you worried about me?"

I love giving him a hard time. It reminds me of simpler times before David ever came to Athens and joined our tight-knit group. Aaron and I used to be the ones having late-night talks when I needed some guy advice or he needed some about Jenny. Phone calls in the middle of the night were a regular thing, then we paired up, and those became less frequent. When David and I split, Aaron became protective again. Calling and checking up on me, asking Jenny how I seemed that day, and so on like we were kids again sitting under the tree in my backyard.

"Would you be mad if I was?" Aaron pulls his best puppy dog eyes.

"Never. I have these two worried as well. I'm used to it." I laugh. "More the merrier is what I always say."

Jenny confidently says, "We aren't too worried."

I whisper to Aaron, "She's totally worried."

He brings the camera to his mouth like a walkie-talkie and whispers, "Only because she loves you."

"Okay, okay, enough whispering you two," Jenny jokes. Then says to Aaron, "Anyway, how's stuff, babe?"

Aaron's face softens. "Good. Same old, same old. Hanging with David. Sorry, Lucy."

"It's okay," I sigh.

"She had another nightmare about David." Jenny spills the beans. So much for not bringing him up again.

I smack my forehead and narrow my eyes. "No need to bring that up. Besides, it was a helpful dream. We all agreed. I'm trying my best. But, what if I'm supposed to—"

Jenny points her finger at me and says, "No, no, you aren't even going there!"

"I didn't even finish. Aaron, Michael, help me." I desperately plead. "I just wanted to have a good day."

"You deserve better advice, Lucy. Not some fake nightmare David fueled by your worries," Jenny scolds. "You deserve more, okay? Yes, I agreed earlier, but I want you to be sure. The bridge is here, and we are crossing it, *now*."

"Well, it's the wrong bridge, but whatever you say." I cross my arms and look at the guys. Wide-eyed and confused, Aaron looks like he wants to say something. "Aaron, do you have something to say? Because I need something, anything, bro."

Aaron chimes in, "How about this? You just focus on your writing and being in Paris. Deal with your feelings, or lack of feelings, for David when you are back in Alabama. Deal?" He pauses, then says, "If you have another dream, y'all work through it calmly. Jenny, I'm talking to you, too."

Jenny sheepishly looks at Aaron. "Sorry for yelling, babe. Lucy, I'm sorry for being harsh. I care about you a lot, and I would rather you be really happy instead of happy for the moment. Healing takes work, and I want to help if that's okay?"

"Remember you have both Michael and Jenny with you, and I am only a phone call away."

Michael says, "Don't forget me, girl. I got your back, too."

I take a deep breath and say, "How hard can it be to focus on my writing when I have amazing helpers."

"You'll always have us," Jenny says. "At this point, David is just a guy you used to love. But we aren't telling you to hate him. We just want you to see that you don't have to run back to him."

"*Exactly.* You don't need him," Michael says. "You have all you need. We just want you to see that, too."

"Anyway," Aaron says, "take me on y'all's walk around the Eiffel Tower. Tell me facts. Lucy, I know you are good at that."

"I do like my facts, yes." I put my hands on my hips. "I'll be the tour guide today. How about that?"

His eyes get big. "Yes, Lucy, tell us what you've learned since getting to Paris."

I look straight into Jenny's camera and say, "Challenge accepted." They all look at me like, *go on, do your nerd thing.* "All right, I've got this. I am a research nerd." I gesture to the amazing, picturesque view. "Jenny, turn the camera to the view so Aaron can look with us, please and thank you."

"I can do that." Then to Aaron, she says, "Ready to see the gorgeous view, babe?"

"Show me Paris!" He hollers and cheers. "Oh, that's beautiful!"

I grin and say, "This is my favorite spot. I could lean on this railing and stare out at the landscape for hours." I point toward the horizon. "Do you see that building directly across from us?"

Aaron hesitates for a second. I glance over and see him squinting. He says, "Barely. What is that, Lucy?"

"Tour Montparnasse, which is a skyscraper with a three-hundred-sixty-degree view over Paris."

Michael says, "The name sounds familiar. Are we going there on this trip?"

I shake my head. "Good guess, but no. We are going to the cemetery nearby, though." To Aaron, I say, "I picked the Montparnasse Cemetery to inspire Michael's poetry skills."

Aaron says, "A little off-roading for your writing?"

"As much as I would love to include the cemetery, it isn't on my topics list. But, that doesn't mean we can't explore more of Paris." I shrug, "Plus, it is really fascinating."

Michael bumps my shoulder and says, "You didn't have to plan a day all for me."

"I sprinkled in tons of places for all three of us." After a beat, I add, "Sometimes I need a break from my writing research."

Jenny says, "Yeah, you and your research are like two peas in a pod. How is that going, by the way?"

"My writing is going well. This extra day at the Eiffel Tower is really helping."

"I'm glad. Which, speaking of the tower, aren't there some other interesting spots on this floor?"

"More than the view, babe?" Aaron says.

"Yes, more than the view."

"Okay, I'm intrigued. Lucy, what's on the top floor?"

"The summit is home to a model of Gustave Eiffel's office, some panoramic maps, the 1889 summit model, and a champagne bar." I roll my eyes. "Of course, you want me to show him the bar." I laugh. "I could go for another glass. We are in Paris, after all."

Aaron says, "She's trying new things. I like this, Lucy."

"I figured it was time to just go with it. I am much better than I was the last few times I was around alcohol."

"I think daring you to drink whiskey is my proudest friend moment!"

"Good thing I was learning to branch out," I say. "It wasn't *all* that bad, at least."

Jenny says, "You took that shot like a champ. Michael, you would have been so proud of her."

Michael says, "I bet I would have. But, for now, let's see her try some white champagne since she tried rosé last time."

I wiggle my brows. "Challenge accepted!"

# CHAPTER 8

# CEMETERY TRIP

———

## AUGUST 29, 2021

Our Converses hit the ground hard as we stepped from a smooth sidewalk to a gray cobblestone walkway with grass growing up through the cracks. The statue in the center of the roundabout catches the morning sun as we enter *Cimetière du Montparnasse*. "The Genius (Angel) of Eternal Sleep" statue guards the hundreds of glamorous and intellectual Parisians who rest in the tombstones and grave plots spanning miles each way. Beautiful colorful flowers decorate the grass. The breeze is cool as we turn toward the tombstones.

Michael's eyes light up as we walk deeper into the cemetery. He sings, "I feel some writing inspiration coming on."

I wiggle my eyebrows and say, "Can we expect spooky poems soon?" His outfit screams horror poet, all-black attire with blood-red shoes. "Are you channeling your inner poet today?"

"Hopefully so." He winks. "Maybe my Edgar Allen Poe attire will help."

Jenny says, "*The Raven* poet, right?"

"The poetry virgin gets it."

"I'm never going to live that down, am I?"

"*Never.*" He chuckles.

I yell, "Okay, okay, break it up. I have major morbid facts to tell y'all." They stare at me. "I read that this is the second-largest cemetery in Paris and the final resting place for only Parisians."

"That is a bit morbid for you. Researching cemeteries for fun. Who are you?"

"Maybe you're rubbing off on me, Sparks." I shrug.

He stops dead in his tracks and looks me straight in the eyes. "Only the strong survive being friends with a horror poet and writer. You must be a strong one, girl."

I dismiss him with the flick of my wrist. "It's nothing."

Jenny says, "Yeah, don't you know who you are talking to? Lucy is the best at this stuff." She bumps my shoulder.

"Thanks, Jen. I guess I just have a knack for loving people for who they are."

"I couldn't have said it better myself."

Michael skips ahead of us, a blur of black and red through the line of crypts, tombs, and grave plots. I shake my head while Jenny and I mosey on behind him in the warm sunshine and cool breeze.

I laugh and say, "Do you think he ever gets winded from skipping?"

"Probably not. He does write about the dead. He's in his element right now." She shrugs, then adds, "How's your article going?"

"It's actually going better than I thought."

She winks. "I told you it would be."

"Yeah, I know. We shall see what the editor thinks when I send it in a few days. But first, I think I will send her an introductory email."

"I think that's a good approach." She links arms with me, and we skip to catch up with Michael.

Out of breath, I manage to call out to him, "Hey, you with the bouncing legs, slow down. You'll wake the dead with those jumps." He keeps bouncing down the cobblestone walkway, gleefully, like a kid in a candy shop. I suppose this is like that for him—morbid, maybe, but true. "Sparks, slow your roll."

As he comes to a halt, we stop in front of an old-time windmill. Faded brown paint covers the building, and it is missing the sails that probably used to spin constantly in the wind. The sun is beaming off the white roof as I squint my eyes to see Michael standing a couple of feet away.

He turns around, hands on his hips and heavily breathing. "Oh, hey gals!"

I yell, "Oh, hey gals, my butt!"

He crouches and says through more heavy breaths. "Sorry, y'all, I was enjoying the breeze and spooky vibes."

I lean on Jenny as I catch my breath. "Well, you better write some poems soon. Plus, I will get to work on finishing my article, with Jenny's help, of course."

Jenny arches her eyebrows and says, "Wait, what could I possibly help you with that the writer best friend can't?"

"He will be busy writing horror poems. Come on, Jen, you always keep me from spiraling into a funnel of self-doubt."

She bumps my hip. "I try."

I smile and turn my attention back to the cemetery. "Sparks, I read that an Irish writer is buried here. I love anything to do with Ireland just as much as Paris."

"You and your research are best friends, Lucy," Michael says, "Let's go find the grave."

Michael stops in front of a line of stone graves—a false tomb. He points to one of the raised stone tombs. "Samuel Beckett lived from 1906 to 1989." His tomb is simple as can be. A gray, rectangular tomb rose a couple of feet from the stone platform under it, with a few flowers at the foot.

Jenny smiles. "How funny that he died the year Taylor Swift was born."

"The greats just know how to line up," I point out.

We stand there for a moment as the breeze gently kisses our faces and tousles our hair. The grounds are quiet and surreal. I take a deep breath as I watch Michael study the gravesites. He carefully makes a note of his surroundings and runs his fingers across the raised print on the gravestones. He types on his phone while Jenny and I quietly look up some more famous resting places. I, at least, want to discover one or two more writers while we are here. Oddly enough, I feel calm as we admire the legends who came before us.

I break the silence. "I found two more writers for us to learn from, Sparks. It says here that they were together for fifty-one years. How sweet they were together for most of their lives."

"I think that is inspirational," Jenny says. "Maybe you can write a poem about love in the afterlife or something?"

He stands up and walks down the cobblestones with us. My toes hit cracks every so often as we look for Jean-Paul Sartre and Simone de Beauvoir's shared gravesite. It can't be too far away, yet this cemetery could serve as a haunted maze.

About ten minutes later, I spot a row of plain, cream tombstones in the shade. Red lipstick prints catch my eye. I tilt my head in confusion and amusement and stare at the tombstone. "Now that's something you don't see every day."

Michael scratches his chin and inspects the lipstick marks. "Who would kiss a grave?"

Jenny ponders, "I guess people really adored them."

"I guess so," I say. "Look they only passed six years apart." Jean-Paul passed in 1980, while his wife passed in 1986.

Michael runs his hand over the smooth stone. "It's just so surreal."

"Spook Master Sparks, do you need a few more minutes with your dead inspirations?"

"I think I am influencing *you* a bit, Lucy."

"Maybe a little bit." I take their hands and start skipping. "I can't wait to see the poetry you pull from today's adventure."


The Paris sky is close to giving way to the nightlife. The sun is high in the sky. We are in a small café waiting to order an early dinner. Between answering emails, writing, a little bit of editing, and getting a head start on researching our next adventure, food won the battle early tonight. I prop my elbows on the table and stare out the window as I think about my editor's email.

Good Afternoon,

I hope this email finds you well. I apologize for the delay in introducing myself to you—the past week has been crazy busy. I'm Lucy Berry, and Ashley Wilson passed along your contact information before I left for Paris. I'll attach my article schedule for good measure.

I have started my Eiffel Tower article. It is coming along nicely. We are even enjoying some extra exploring, such as bookstores, libraries, and cemeteries.

I look forward to hearing your thoughts as this journey begins.

Thanks,
Lucy Berry


Hello Ms. Berry,

I'm doing well. I hope you are, too. No need to apologize for the delay. I'm Judith Garcia, and it's very nice to meet you, Ms. Berry. Ashley has told me good things about you, and I look forward to working with you.

I'm a remote editor working from my home state (Arkansas) currently. Therefore, all corresponding with my team is over email or Zoom. *Getaway Travel Magazine* headquarters is in the Eastern Time Zone (Pennsylvania)—an hour ahead of CST and six ahead of you.

Concerning your article due dates:

On September 5 (and further dates), email your articles at 7:00 a.m. CST/2:00 p.m. CEST with your article in a Google Document. I plan on keeping you involved with the editing so we can learn together what works and what doesn't and keep strengthening your writing through this first assignment.

I look forward to hearing from you. If you ever have any questions, don't hesitate to send me a quick email. I am more than happy to help.

Best,
Judith Garcia
Editor in Chief
*Getaway Travel Magazine*


Jenny says, "Michael, did you get your spook on yet?"

He smolders and stares off into the distance. "I might have whipped up two short horror poems today."

I smile and say, "Sparks, wow us with your horror poems, please and thank you."

"Yes, yes, Mr. Spook Master Sparks," Jenny cheers. "We want to know the spooky realms of your mind."

He grins grimly and scratches his chin.

"Well—l—l!" I prompt him.

"Oh, y'all want me to read them." He pauses. "Well, of course." He clears his throat. "The first one is called, 'Living in the Air.'"

"*Oh,*" Jenny and I say together.

*Dealing cards in the*
*evening provokes mystery.*
*a bird with fire—*
*the phoenix*
*humming and swinging in the air.*

Jenny beams. "Man, you are incredible! Also, I love the imagery."

I say, "Someone has been picking up on writing terms and such."

"One must flow with the ways of her friends' interests." She winks.

"Well, whatever it may be, I think you nailed it."

"It's hard to miss the imagery. His poem is light, but also dark and mysterious."

"Oh, so true." I analyze the imagery, "I love how it shows a phoenix hovering above the night, like a watcher."

"The first two lines remind me how we may deal cards, but the end result will always be a mystery. Like saying deal if you dare, but you may not like what you find."

"I love that depiction. Then he bookends it with the phoenix watching overhead. Like ghosts hover in a cemetery, the phoenix flies overhead and hums a spooky song."

Michael props his hands on his chin and gushes, "I love y'all."

"We love you, too," we singsong.

"Would y'all like to hear the other poem?"

We both eagerly nod.

He proceeds without hesitation. "This one is called, 'Cemetery Sleeps.'" Michael clears his throat again. The café feels like a poetry reading. The streetlights cast a heavy shadow across his face. Night sets in over the city.

*Tears fall, sadness overwhelms, death reigns.*
*When it rains, the ground sinks. Flowers feign*
*and replenish. Rain gives them life*
*even when everyone who has survived await a certain strife.*
*What was once a place where darkness surrounds,*
*our ancestors are at rest year-round.*

Snaps all around. We step onto the sidewalk, and the cool breeze sends chill bumps down my arms. The sky turns darker. We head back to the hotel as our stomachs, hearts, and minds overflow with the adventures of the day.

# CHAPTER 9

# THE LOUVRE

---

## SEPTEMBER 2, 2021

Four days later, I prop my elbow on the taxi's backseat window. The sun is gleaming on the Seine River. We cross the bridge to the business side of Paris. Our taxi driver says, "We will arrive at the Louvre shortly."

The Louvre is the world's largest museum and a historic monument in Paris. They have one of the most impressive art collections, which contains pieces from famous artists such as Leonardo da Vinci. The *Mona Lisa* has been heavily guarded and protected since 2005 when it was moved to the Louvre's largest room.

We step onto the curb about a hundred yards from the beautiful glass pyramid. The sun blinds me as rays ping off the pyramid's point. The light is casting heavy shadows on the pavement. I spot the entrance sign, and we pay for our tickets. I grab a map and flip through the pages. "I want to find the *Mona Lisa*."

Michael leans over my shoulder and says, "Where is it?"

Jenny says, "Are you thinking of making that the focus of your article?"

"It's on the Denon Wing's first floor." I stumble over my words a bit. "I think I do. I've always admired da Vinci's art."

"It would make a great focus," Jenny encourages me as we head to the painting's room. "Something to draw the readers to the Louvre."

"Most definitely."


The glass case is illuminated by its own LED lamp. A wooden railing keeps viewers from touching the protective casing, with no chance for fingerprints. The *Mona Lisa* is prim and proper even after more than five hundred years following completion. Held by a wooden frame, the woman is magnificent and enchanting. She looks into the distance, almost feeling like she's staring at the audience. The backdrop is faded, a mountain view with rolling hills, rigid canyons, and forest pines against a blue and yellow sky. We cram in between people as the crowd thickens around us.

"So, Lucy Lu, tell us about the famous *Mona Lisa*," Jenny prompts. "We know you researched beforehand."

"Oh, you know I have something up my sleeve." I wink and read my notes app. "The *Mona Lisa* was stolen in 1911 and wasn't recovered until 1913."

"Wait, is that why it's in a glass case?"

Michael chimes in, "Well, it is famous." He has a point, but that's not the only reason.

"It's a Leonardo da Vinci original," I say. "The glass is also bulletproof—one very secure and protected painting, I'll say."

"The painting is more protected than the president."

Jenny says, "Does it have its own guards?"

"Indeed it does." Her jaw drops, and I continue, "I guess they wanted to be certain that no one could steal it again."

"That's bonkers." She shakes her head in disbelief.

"Think of it this way—it's just as important as the Declaration of Independence."

Michael says, "Of course you'd reference the Nicolas Cage movie, *National Treasure?*"

"She knows it's one of my favorite history movies." Jenny grins. "We actually watched it with her parents a couple of times."

"My family loves *National Treasure.*" I remember those nights as if they were just yesterday. "Our family movie nights pretty much consist of Nicolas Cage films."

"How much does your family love it?" Michael raises his eyebrows.

"Just as much as people love the *Mona Lisa.*"

His mouth forms an O.

"How can one not love figuring out the past?" I ponder. "Like how famous artists came up with their most memorable pieces. It is all so fascinating."

Jenny admires the painting. She tilts her head and says, "I wonder why someone would want to steal another person's creation? I would be devastated if someone jacked my drawings."

"Probably a greedy person without a care in the world," Michael scoffs.

"You aren't far off." I scroll through my notes. "I found out that a former Louvre glazier tried to sell the *Mona Lisa* to an art dealer."

"An art dealer? Glazier? That's terrible." Jenny crosses her arms. A few people squeeze past us. I forgot for a second that we are in a massive crowd.

I shake my head. "This article is going to be a doozy. So many details to keep track of."

"You'll be great." Michael comforts me. "How did your editor sound? Nice, rude, or somewhere in between?"

"She sounded nice. I'm just nervous about sharing my thoughts with that many people." I let out a heavy breath. "These aren't just blogs about my feelings. These are articles about four well-known Paris locations." I stare at the painting and wonder how Leonardo fought self-doubt or if he ever wanted to throw in the paintbrush.

Jenny pats my shoulder. "Michael and I are right here with you. The writer and art history buff have your back. The editing feedback can only destroy you if you let it."

Michael pats my other shoulder. The simple touch calms me. "Worry is inevitable, but how we choose to overcome it says a lot about us. I believe you'll do just fine when that time comes." They squeeze me, and we agree to keep moving forward. If a five-hundred-year-old painting can withstand the storms, so can I.

I stare at the painting, making mental notes of all the small details. From the distant look in her eyes to the wrinkles in her sleeves, the woman is almost lifelike. She watches her audience with distinct concern and admiration as they take in her beauty. She isn't done up in fancy clothes or jewels but resembles the likes of a wealthy girl making her way in this world. I quickly type out a few details and round them out to complete sentences. Maybe this will be the start of my article. Maybe making her the focus will make my article pop but also challenge me to dig deep into the wonders of art.

"I hope my editor likes my article," I say, half to myself, and sigh.

Jenny nods and says, "All you can do is your best." She adds, "Look at it this way. You are putting yourself out there just like the legends."

"I don't know if I'm like the legends, but I do hope I make an impact on at least one person."

"Every legend started out small." Michael bumps my hip. "They keep climbing. Will you?"

"Look at you two dropping wisdom." I smile. "I'm going to keep going even when self-doubt overflows and my dreams seem out of reach. I'm going to keep pushing like the greats did before me."

"That's our girl," they cheer.

We squeeze our way out of the ever-growing *Mona Lisa* crowd and walk around the rest of the room. All the while, I am daydreaming about how I will incorporate my thoughts and research into such a well-known museum and painting. I push the wonders away and enjoy the rest of the museum.

# CHAPTER 10

# THE BERRY'S

_____

## SEPTEMBER 2, 2021

After walking around the Louvre, we hailed a taxi back to the hotel. I plop on the bed face-first. My feet tingle. I press my face into the mattress, trying to ignore the sharp pains. "My feet hurt so much, and I want to take a long, long nap."

The mattress moves beside me. Jenny says, "Don't forget you promised to check in with your parents today." I raise my head and glare at her. She pokes my sides and begs, "Come on. I love Momma B and Mr. B. FaceTime them so we can all catch up."

I rise up on my knees, grab my phone, and call my parents. "Honey, honey, can you hear us?" My parents say loudly into the camera, but I can only see the top of their heads.

"Mom, Dad, back up so I can see your faces."

"Is this better, honey?" Mom asks as their faces come into view.

"I can see y'all much better."

"Oh, good, sweetie. How are you? How are Jenny and Michael? How is Paris?" She exhales deeply as she catches her breath.

I smile. "I'm doing really well." I pan my camera to Jenny, and she waves, then to Michael, who waves as his eyes look like they might close any second. "They are doing good. You know, keeping me from getting lost or behind on writing—the normal things. Paris is incredible. I still can't believe we're here." I pause for a moment, "We visited the Louvre today."

"That's good to hear. How was the museum?"

"I loved it. Seeing the *Mona Lisa* up close was a dream come true."

"It sounds like one." She smiles her big smile that says she's happy for me, then adds, "You've already been gone a week."

"It is going by so fast," I remind her.

"Not for the ones here in the States. I miss my baby." My mom pokes out her bottom lip.

"Dad, tell Mom to stop pouting. I'll be home before she knows it."

Dad rolls his eyes like we are the most ridiculous people ever. "You two will be okay apart for a couple more weeks, hon." He rubs my mom's shoulder and kisses her on the cheek.

My mom huffs, "I know, I know. She's grown."

"I am, and you taught me well. I've got this." I place my hand on my heart. "I promise."

Jenny pops into the frame and says, "And if she doesn't, we have her back, Momma B."

My mom gushes, "Thanks, sweetie. I know y'all take good care of each other."

"We stick together."

"We really do!" I smile, then ask, "So how is everything and everyone at home?"

"Everything and everyone are doing good. Just missing you, honey."

I hesitate. "So, no news on anything? And I miss everyone, too."

"Oh, we know what you're asking about, dear," my dad says. I can't hide anything from him. My parents look at each other, and I try to read their facial expressions.

"David has stopped by a few times to see how we are," my mom admits. "He was like a son for so long. I didn't have the heart to turn him away." She quickly adds, "I don't like slamming the door in people's faces."

I scrunch up my nose. "What happened? And I know, Mom, I know. I understand your reasoning. I don't feel the same, but I understand." I try my best to hide the hurt, but I am not too surprised. My parents loved David. The situation makes sense. As an afterthought, I ask, "Did Aaron tell him I was on a trip?"

Dad says, "In our brief exchange, he said that Aaron briefly mentioned that you were out of the country with Jenny."

"Mom, is that *all*, or is there something else?"

"He was checking in on you," she hesitates, then blurts out. "He still cares. Before you say it, yes, I was shocked, but he said it."

I take a minute to get words out. "If, *if*, he cared about me, he wouldn't have proposed to Alice or cheated on me in the first place!"

"Honey, I know, but I'm just telling you what he said. That's all." She lets out a breath. "We are on your side, but we also want you to see that moving on from him is important too. I was mad as can be when he wronged you, but I can't hold that hate in my heart forever. At some point, you just have to let go and live for you. We want you to be happy."

"Yes, yes, I know. I'm the one who asked." I take a breath to gather my thoughts, then add, "How could you not turn him away? I know you said you didn't have the heart. I just don't understand after everything that happened."

"Judging him isn't our place, sweetie," Dad says. "Yes, our forgiveness came a little sooner than yours, but that doesn't mean we support you any less or agree with his actions. Does that make sense?"

I pick at a scab on my knee. "You want me to see that it is possible to heal my wounds?"

They both grin. Dad says, "You're learning, sweetie. You'll get there with time." He lovingly says, "Just to clarify, it was a very brief conversation on the porch a few times. We would never betray you by condoning his actions, but we also don't want to be rude to others either. It's a tricky situation, I know. We just want to see you happy again no matter what he's up to or who he talks to."

Jenny says, "She really is making progress."

"I really am."

My mom says, "Have the dreams stopped?"

"They aren't as frequent."

"Any progress is good progress."

"Very true," I say, "I think I'm going to catch some z's."

"Get some rest, honey."

"We'll talk soon, dear. Call or text whenever," Dad says.

"I will. I love and miss y'all."

"We love and miss you, too, honey. Take care."

"Take care."

Jenny looks over at me as I put my phone on the charger. "You okay, Lucy Lu?"

Propping my head on my arm, I sigh and say, "It happens. I can't stop what he feels, you know?"

She gives me sad eyes and says, "That's true. I mean, I told you when you invited him over that day that he still cared.

Plus, he felt so bad for hurting you. But that doesn't excuse his actions." She shakes her head. "You could have given him another chance, but I still stand by Michael's point that David could have done it again."

"I'm actually glad I didn't give him another chance," I confidently say.

"Trust me. You aren't missing out," she laughs. "He has Aaron, Alice, and the guys. You have Michael, Aaron, and me, which is much better."

"Yeah. Like I said a few weeks ago, just because he lost his wife doesn't mean he has to lose his best friend, too. He and Aaron are best buds, you know?"

"Oh, I know. They had some guys' nights after it all blew up, and they drank whiskey and carried on like teenagers." She rolls her eyes. "Honestly, that's probably what they've been doing since I left. You know how Aaron gets lonely."

"They really do keep each other company."

"The bromance is real."


I jolt straight up in bed, suddenly wide awake. My whole body is burning up. I fling the heavy comforter off and fan my face. Sweat drips down my forehead.

Another nightmare. I thought I was past this already. My conscience had other plans.

Without fully opening her eyes, Jenny says, "Lucy, my dear, sweet Lucy, what are you doing?" She takes a deep breath, opens her eyes, and looks at me. Her face softens. "What time is it?"

"Sorry I woke you up. I was burning up." I fan my face again. "It's a little after seven."

She perks up. "Want to go watch the sunset at the Eiffel Tower?"

"Stop for macarons, too?"

Our giddy laughter wakes Michael. We are all up and ready in twenty minutes. We fly out the hotel's double doors onto the sidewalk. Suddenly, I feel a ping in my chest. I lied about my nightmare again. I need to confess the truth about why I woke up so suddenly. Tell them it wasn't just because I was burning up. As the Eiffel Tower comes into view, I battle my inner thoughts.

*They are going to yell at me.*

*Jenny's going to be so mad.*

*I should have never asked my parents about him.*

*I should have left him behind like he left me.*

*I should confess. I need to confess.*

*Healing begins with me spilling my guts.*

Michael tilts his head and says, "Lucy, are you okay?"

"I had yet another nightmare about David." I bite my bottom lip.

Jenny slightly snaps, "I thought the dreams stopped? I mean, we just told your mom."

"I thought so, but apparently, that was a premature thought. Even dream-David was confused." I twist a piece of hair around my finger—tighter and tighter.

Michael scoffs, "Wait, what did he say this time?"

The Paris street nightlife is almost upon us. I check the time. We only have fifteen minutes until sunset. The lawn is packed. Blankets and people fill almost every patch of grass. Luckily, we manage to squeeze between two larger families. "He asked me why he was still in my dreams and if I had listened to his advice from the last time."

"I thought you had?"

"I did," I whine. "He also asked if I had recently talked about him." I fan the blanket out. "He got me good there.

We discussed him briefly on FaceTime earlier. Then, Jenny and I continued for a bit afterward." I smack my forehead. "I am so dumb."

Jenny puts her hands on her hips and glares at me. She stomps her foot and hollers, "You are *not* dumb, Lucy Matilda! Don't you ever let him or anyone make you feel that way!"

My jaw drops.

Michael says, "Your middle name is Matilda?"

I scowl at Jenny. "Yeah, but no one ever uses it!"

She puts her hands up in surrender. "I only use your middle name when necessary."

I roll my eyes.

"I love your middle name," Michael reassures me. "Matilda is a beautiful name."

"My mom was obsessed with the book for years before I was born."

"I can see where you get your love of references from."

Jenny bumps me. "Lucy is just like her mom."

"No one else I would rather take after." I grin, feeling better. "My movie references are my quirk."

"I will always love your references."

"Me too!" Michael gives me a hard high five.

"Good, because y'all are stuck with them."

We all burst out laughing. The sky changes colors from a deep orange to pitch black. We munch on our macaroons.

I melt into the moment, forgetting my worries as the lights illuminate the city.

# CHAPTER 11

# APPROACHING DEADLINE

---

## SEPTEMBER 5, 2021

Paris is magical. In the last week or so, we've seen the city from the highest point, we've viewed one of the most famous paintings, and been to the prettiest park. I drag myself out of bed. Only sixteen days left on our trip. It is going by so fast. I don't want it to end. My Eiffel Tower article is due today, so it's crunch time before I send it to my editor this afternoon. I fake crack my knuckles and open my laptop. I click on my Google document and start reading.

*The Eiffel Tower is a French Monument and the brainchild of Gustave Eiffel, whose office set still occupies a place on the top (summit) floor. Gustave Eiffel built his incredible design to celebrate the 1889 Exposition Universelle. The event for the competition commemorates the one-hundredth anniversary of the French Revolution.*

My opening line is actually decent. Off to a good start, I'll say. My layout mirrors the tower's structure, one level at a time. I pay close attention to how they work together and how different the levels are. I emphasize why tourists should visit every level and take their time. After all, this is an experience of a lifetime.

Jenny's alarm goes off, and both she and Michael stir. I turn in my chair to face them. "Good morning, sunshines!"

Jenny groans and says, "Why are you so cheery this early?" She scowls at me.

"We are in Paris, silly. There is plenty to be happy about right now."

"I just want to re-enter my dream world."

"I can guarantee the real world is better."

She rolls her eyes. "You have a point. What do you think, Michael?"

He sleepily says, "Yeah, whatever Lucy said. Let's go with that. It is always good."

"The man has spoken."

"I've been up for hours." I lay my head on the backrest of the chair and stared at them. "I'm almost done with my article."

"Aren't you just adorable?" He sits up. "Are you sending it in soon?"

I put my hands under my chin and grin. "Yes, hopefully." I look back at my screen.

"How much more do you need to edit?"

"I want to make sure I've exhausted everything before I send it. You know?" I sigh. "Does that make sense?"

Jenny says, "You want to put as much into the article as possible before you let someone pick it apart, right?"

"Yes. You always understand me."

"It's my job." She smiles. "How about you finish up, then we'll hit the mall for some retail therapy."

"More like window shopping," I reply. "I'm in."

For the next hour, I go through my draft with a fine-tooth comb. No typos or odd sentences are making it to the editor's desk. I've got this. I am busy taking fluff out left and right while Jenny and Michael snooze behind me. They couldn't resist their dream world. I crank out a few more sentences before my eyes start stinging. I rub at my eyes and make the call—my editor can handle it from here. I type out a quick email, attach my Google Doc, and crawl back in bed to rest my eyes.

Good Morning,

I hope this email finds you doing well. I am excited to send you my first Paris article, "A Glimpse at the Eiffel Tower."

I look forward to hearing from you.
Talk soon.
Thanks,
Lucy Berry

The city flies past my window. We steadily zoom down the narrow streets. Crossing over the Seine River, our taxi takes a right onto a small side street. I press my face against the glass like a little kid. I am taken back to family car rides. My parents loved blasting eighties music and seeing how many different state licenses they could spot. I always lost. To me, they were geniuses and superheroes. I never went on trips without them—until now.

Our taxi slowly parks in front of the open staircase, the entrance to the Westfield Forum des Halles Shopping Mall. I am speechless at how massive the mall is. Tall and narrow clear glass windows line the curves in the building's elegant structure. Sunlight streams through the canopy roof, which has a striking resemblance to the Louvre's pyramid. Instead of tiny triangles, the mall's roof is made up of long, gold waves flowing from one side to another.

Hooking my arms through Michael's and Jenny's, we head into the belly of the mall.

My face lights up at the familiar yellow sign as we walk up to the LEGO Store. My feet halt in front of the wide display windows that hold colorful LEGO bricks in various shapes and sizes. The memory smacks me in between the eyes.

Jenny says, "What's that look for?"

"You are going to hate it."

She raises her eyebrows. One is twitching. "Oh, I see. Is it a David memory?"

"An old one from a weekend trip to Nashville." I give a melancholy smile. "Yes, it's a good one. Maybe even funny and memorable."

David moved from Nashville to Athens, Alabama, when we were high school freshmen. His dad had been promoted to manager of an ever-growing window company, and he was reassigned to run the Alabama store. David loved being my tour guide when we came to see his aunt and uncle sometimes.

"The memory includes the LEGO Store?"

Michael says, "Yeah, that's a little strange, even for me."

"Strange but still funny." I shrug.

Jenny waves her hand. "So, what's the funny memory?"

"Right. Right after David and I graduated from college, we went on a weekend trip. We went to the mall on our first day. You know, Opry Mills?"

"I love that mall. Everyone raves about it."

I remember that day like it was yesterday. We were young and madly in love. We couldn't keep our hands off each other. My arm looped through his as we walked around the mall. We did more window shopping than purchasing that day.

"It's because they have everything." I nudge them. "I bet this place does, too."

Michael says, "Lucy, you're getting sidetracked."

"Oh, right, sorry." I blush. "Where was I?"

"Y'all came to Opry Mills on your first day."

"We were window shopping and making tons of loops around the mall. We were cracking jokes and laughing. Having fun together. On one of our final loops, we stopped in front of the LEGO Store. Much like we are right now. He leaned into me and whispered, 'If you let me go in there, you'll never get me out.' Apparently, LEGO bricks were his weakness."

The twinkle in his eyes, jokester grin, and charm that could swoon me for days play in my mind. We're laughing about his secret obsession with building LEGO bricks. Him pulling me toward the store's door, and me pulling him back into the crowd. We can't go in, or we'll never make it to lunch. Jenny's voice pulls me back to the here and now. I shrug off the need to enter the store. Instead, I look at the display window just like David and I did in Nashville all those years ago.

"Apparently, LEGO bricks were his weakness," Jenny shrugs, "but I never heard him mention it."

"Maybe it was his hidden identity." Michael coughs. "He did turn out to be a villain. Man, his story actually started out good."

David was this wholesome Southern boy from Nashville who loved me so much. Looking back, I would have never guessed he would cheat on me. To this day, he was a good guy turned evil.

"He probably did have a secret identity." Jenny sees my face fall and adds, "Hey, it isn't your fault, Lucy Lu. Plus, you seem happy, no tears?"

"He isn't worth my tears." I cross my arms. "Sometimes, the best of people turn into villains."

It is okay to be happy about a memory because it's only a moment in time. I push forward toward the staircase, bypassing the LEGO Store and heading toward the future. I am slowly learning to grow through the memories that randomly pop up. Without those situations, I wouldn't be who I am now. His presence in my life wasn't by mistake. He existed to make me better, and I left to meet myself again. He was only a chapter in my life, not my whole story. I am done hating myself for remembering my past. Instead, I choose to be thankful.

We descend deeper into the mall with our arms tightly linked together. One step at a time while we try not to fall. I grab onto the railing as Jenny starts wiggling. She says, "Okay, I can't walk like this. Unlink arms until we are off these stairs!"

I let go of their arms and took a few more steps down. "Better?"

Jenny dramatically stretches her arms, walks down the steps to me, and says, "Oh yes, much better."

Michael rolls his eyes. "You two are too funny. Do y'all know that?"

Jenny and I look at each other and say simultaneously. "We know!"

"First LEGO Stores, now walking on steps. What's next?"

"The possibilities are endless," Jenny says and skips down the rest of the steps.

I look at Michael. "I guess we should join her?"

"Probably so. Don't want her wandering off," Michael says.

Hello Ms. Berry,

Thank you so much for being early on the deadline. I greatly appreciate it. As of right now, we are planning to have your article ready for publication on September 10, 2021. As soon as the article link is available, I will send it over to you to easily share with whomever you wish.

Here are my thoughts on editing:

Today (September 5): I look over your article and start content and mechanical editing.

Tomorrow (September 6): Finalize my edits by 9:00 a.m. (CDT)/4:00 p.m. (CEST).

September 8: Email me your edited Google Document at Noon (CDT)/7:00 p.m. (CEST).

September 8 (later that day here): Your article will be with the head of the team—making sure it goes up on the website in time.

My game plan is to only do one round of editing, but that can change. If it does, just keep an eye on your email. Concerning this article, if another edit is needed, I will send it on September 9 (4:00 p.m. CEST).

In the meantime, I hope your second article is going well. Email me if you have any questions.

Best,
Judith Garcia
Editor in Chief
*Getaway Travel Magazine*


I read my email highlights aloud. "My article will be published on the tenth. That's five days away. She's starting editing now and will have them ready tomorrow at four. Wow!"

Michael says, "That's doable. Jenny and I can help."

Jenny nods and says, "Between the three of us, we can hit deadlines."

"You have a little over twenty-four hours before you'll have the edits so, let's continue exploring. How about that?"

I take a couple of deep breaths. *I love deadlines and little wait, but that was a lot at one time.* I center my mind and relax a little bit. I say, "Sounds like a plan. Sometimes writing is hard."

Michael says, "You have a very good point."

"It must be so hard being writers." Jenny jokes, then grabs our hands. "All right, writers, let's go!"

# CHAPTER 12

# RODIN MUSEUM

———

## SEPTEMBER 9, 2021

We venture into a quiet museum with a lively Parisian history and charm. Greenery and wide sidewalks lead us to the mansion-like building. Complete with tower-style endcaps and long, oval-shaped windows, I feel like we stepped into Taylor Swift's "Blank Space" music video. The property is only missing a galloping majestic white horse.

Jenny says, "What did Google tell you about the Rodin Museum?"

I grin and say, "Google told me that this museum is dedicated to the works by Auguste Rodin, which is why it is named the Rodin Museum."

Auguste Rodin, a French sculptor, was unlike any other sculptor during his time. He tested the bounds of how viewers should perceive art. He crafted his sculptures with deep emotions of the mind, such as tragedy and joy, to escalate the human brain. It is said that he paved the way for modern sculpture. Although his work wasn't well-known until his forties, he made a major impact on the art community in Paris when he donated all his life's work to the museum a year before his passing.

"Oh, nice!" Michael says. "Any suggestions on what artwork we should look for?"

We are in the museum's lobby as I look at a Paris blog. "Ah, so these are the artworks I am considering for my article: *The Thinker, The Kiss, The Gates of Hell, Fall of Illusion: Sister of Icarus*, and *Age of Maturity*." I take a breath and continue, "Then we can just go anywhere in the museum."

"You are the tour guide, Ms. Lucy."

Jenny rolls her eyes and says, "Yes, Ms. Lucy, you are the tour guide."

I stand on my tippy-toes. "Why yes, I am. Let's go look at some amazing art."

A few minutes later, we are in the garden area, admiring Rodin's attention to detail. The artwork in front of us looks familiar. I can't put my finger on where I have seen it, though. I tilt my head to the side and walk closer to see the nameplate, *The Thinker*. I turn to my history expert and say, "Hey, Jen, was this sculptor in a movie or something? It looks familiar."

"It was."

"And that movie is?"

Michael says, "If I may interrupt this history movie moment. Lucy, how don't you know this movie? You live and breathe movies."

"He got you there, gal."

"All right, let me *think*."

"Good pun, good pun," Michael says.

"Why, thank you, I thought really hard about it." I pull my best-thinking face. I know this movie. I used to watch it all the time in college, almost as much as *Hocus Pocus*.

"I bet you did, Ms. Tour Guide." Michael winks.

"That's me." I beam as the answer is on the tip of my tongue.

"Do you know what movie it is, or am I going to have to spill the beans?" Jenny teases.

"Double feature, history theme, and *The Thinker*. Meaning it took place in a museum, right? It is on the tip of my tongue." I smack my forehead. "Of course, it's a Ben Stiller movie."

"You are so close. Think hard."

"*Night at the Museum: Battle of The Smithsonian.*"

"Bingo!" She high-fives me. "Where to next?"

"Further into the Sculpture Garden." I point toward the blocks of bushes. "More art awaits us."

Greenery as tall as *The Thinker* surrounds us. Four openings lead us to the other parts of this beautiful outside area. As soon as we emerge from the tunnel of bushes, I whisper, "Are you ready to see *The Gates of Hell*?"

"Uh, hm, are you," Michael whispers, "*The Reaper*?"

I lower my voice. "What if I am?" Halloween is coming early this year.

His eyes widen as if they are going to pop out of his head. His Adam's apple bobbles. He squeaks out, "Take me to your gates, please."

I straighten up, looking from Michael to the other side of the Sculpture Garden sections. I extend my arm, rolling out my fingers and joints. "This way, my dear friends." We come face to face with the incredibly detailed gate. I give them a daunting side-eye. "Welcome to *The Gates of Hell*."

Michael whispers, "It's a nice gate. Is that bronze, by chance?"

Making the horror master sweat is generally amusing. He could have been an actor in another life. I smile as he gazes at the masterpiece, bronze and gleaming in the morning sun.

"The fire pathway must start with a bronze seal. It makes it classier that way." I lean into him, a hair below a whisper, and add, "All the horror kings loved bronze, and they know you will, too."

"If all the horror kings want me to go, then I must go," Michael bravely says. "I must be with my fellow spooky masters of the night." He reaches out his hand, only inches away from the incredibly detailed bronze sculpture.

"They really want you to join them," I bellow. "Can't you hear their whispers?"

He shifts his eyes. "They want me to be their new leader. I must go." His body goes rigid, and in a grave tone, he says, "The current king is telling me that he wants to step down and make me their leader. I don't make the rules, my dear sweet friends. I am dark and dangerous. They need me there."

I grab his shoulder. "I can't let you go. I'm sorry there's been a mistake. Are you Mr. Dark?"

"No. I'm Mr. Sparks?"

"I'm sorry, wrong guy. Although, the horror kings want you down there as their leader, it isn't your time yet."

His eyes go hollow. "Honestly, the best horror king is still alive anyway."

"Is that you, sir?"

"No, that's Stephen King. The only true horror king I'm interested in meeting."

"I've heard of him. A good man and an incredible horror author. I'm not sure he'll fit down there anyway. You'll have better luck with Earth."

"That's the one. Maybe I'll get to meet him. I'm glad you have the wrong man." He takes a deep breath. "I'm Mr. Sparks, and I'll stay right here with my friends if that's okay?"

"As you wish, my kind sir." I grin and say, "And... *scene!*"

"You're a really convincing Reaper, Lucy," Jenny says. "I'm not sure if I should be scared or not."

"Oh, you know I have my ways. Plus, Michael plays along great with my improv moments."

"I wouldn't have it any other way." He laughs and shoves my shoulder.

We stare at the bronze gates. The masterpiece offers such intricate and varied works. We don't move for several moments. Rodin must have put so much time into each small figure. "I know it is supposed to look like gates, but it reminds me of a wardrobe." I tap my chin. "Narnia?"

Jenny steps back a few inches to get a better look. She says, "Could be. Maybe we should have opened it." She giggles. "What do you think, Michael?"

"They both represent going into a different world," he agrees. "But I'm still not opening that door."

"The underworld or Narnia? I would pick Narnia, ten times over," I admit.

He smirks. "We really are book nerds, aren't we?" He runs his hand on the back of his neck. "I'd pick Narnia any day. The horror kings can wait."

"Hm, duh." I point to the space between the top of the doors. "Hey, that's *The Thinker*!"

"That *Thinker* sure is important."

Jenny says, "It is one of his most well-known figures."

With her art and history background, Jenny is in her element. Back in Alabama, she may be a history professor, but one of her many passions includes art. When I was picking these adventures, I wanted to include places that all of us could easily love, plus they are my main audience with my writing. When I am struggling to write about something major, such as a famous art piece, I know I can bounce my ideas off them.

I say, "Have you come across it other than in the Ben Stiller movie?"

"I came across it in my art history course first year of college, I believe, or at least around that time. I know that *The Thinker* was one of the figures that stood out the most to Rodin while he was crafting *The Gates of Hell* sculpture."

"It definitely had to be important to be one of the figures that are not only mounted on another sculpture but also its own."

"Exactly!" Jenny exclaims. "Are you planning on centering your article around the figures that connect to *The Gates of Hell*?"

"What do you know, missy? I looked into all the sculptures, but I need more clarity, Professor Morgan."

Michael says, "You are about to get schooled, Lucy."

"Okay, so you listed off *The Thinker* and *The Kiss,* which are both included in *The Gates of Hell.* Then, you also listed off the *Fall of Illusion: Sister of Icarus,* which is tricky. Some think the idea came to Rodin while he was creating the figures for the gates, but others won't give any clue as to if the sculpture was originally included or not. Mostly, my point is that Rodin drew from one subject matter for a lot of his works, and that would be neat to see in your article."

"And she schooled you!" Michael's mouth forms an O.

She waves her hand. "Sometimes I just know things, that's all."

I give them a tiny smile. "It is true. Sometimes she just knows things right then and there. I've always admired that about her."

Two hours later, we are sitting in a small café a couple of blocks from the museum. The afternoon hustle and bustle is setting in outside the four glass-panel windows. The sun is casting a harsh shadow on the nearby walls as we scan the lunch menu. My phone buzzing on the table interrupts my thoughts.

Hello Ms. Berry,

I wanted to give you the heads-up that your article is set to come out tomorrow afternoon. I will send the link over as soon as I can.

Much to my joy, your article didn't need a second round of editing. Great work and I look forward to reading more from you soon.

Best,
Judith Garcia
Editor in Chief
*Getaway Travel Magazine*

I squeal with excitement. They stare at me. I take a couple of deep breaths and say, "The second round of editing wasn't needed for my Eiffel Tower article. It is coming out tomorrow!"

Jenny drops her menu. "You're kidding."

"No!"

Michael lays his menu down and says, "Let me see that email."

I turn my phone to him as quickly as I can. "See, see. I nailed that piece."

He high-fives me. "Girl, I knew you could do it." He waves a finger between him and Jenny. "We knew you could do it."

"We knew this before the trip, but you keep on outdoing yourself, Lucy Lu."

"I don't know about outdoing myself, but I did surprise myself."

"We are celebrating by ending the day at the Eiffel Tower," Michael says.

"Our favorite spot."

"With our favorite treats."

"Macaroons."

Soft lines replace the once-harsh afternoon sunlight as the sky slowly starts to change to nighttime. The crowded lawn is silent. The air is cool and breezy—a perfect September evening in Paris. Shifting a little to get the feeling back in my feet, I am calm. "This is the moment that makes all the struggles worth it."

Michael bumps my shoulder. "No better way to end the night than right here, and tomorrow you'll have an article published. All your hardships have led you to this moment."

"Wise words from a very wise man."

"I'm flattered."

Jenny says, "You are very wise for your young age."

"And so are you, Jenny. You made professor before the age of twenty-six. How neat is that token?"

"I am beyond blessed they hired me. Plus, I get all this time to school you two."

"Ah, yes. No better way to spend your time off than with two writers in a foreign country."

"No better way."

"Lucy, just think. Tomorrow you'll be legit, and this whole trip will be even more exciting," Michael says.

"A published writer," I muse. "More than just my blog, wow, that's big."

"Very big. We need to find some wine tomorrow to celebrate."

"I'm always down for wine."

"Y'all know I am." Jenny grins.

"Tomorrow, we celebrate with wine and more exploring." Michael raises his final macaroon in the air. "Lucy, I propose that you don't write until tomorrow evening."

I lightly tap my chin with my index finger. "Now that is a movement that I can get behind. Tomorrow is a new and exciting day, y'all. I am ready."

We fall silent as the crowd thins out, and nighttime life is upon us. We roll up our blanket and make our short walk back to our hotel. The Eiffel Tower is a beacon of light and hope. It stands as the city's centerpiece, the main attraction that brings people from all over the world. If it weren't for my strong love for the iron structure, I don't know how our trip would have started out. Because I have this overwhelming desire in my soul to learn everything about anything, but especially the Eiffel Tower. It was the reason that initially drew me to Paris because when I had no hope, the tower gave me my spark back. I think Paris is as magical as the movies depict.

# CHAPTER 13

# FIRST TRAVEL ARTICLE

———

## SEPTEMBER 10, 2021

Hello Ms. Berry,

The day has finally arrived. Your first article is live on the website. I am so excited to move forward in this writing journey with you.

Do you have any questions about your Louvre article? I hope you enjoyed the Rodin Museum trip. It is definitely an adventure of one of the best French artists.

Here's your Eiffel Tower article link: https://www.getawaytravelmag.com/a-glimpse-at-the-eiffel-tower.

Best,
Judith Garcia
Editor in Chief
*Getaway Travel Magazine*

Hello Mrs. Garcia,

Thank you so much. I am thrilled to have my first article up. It looks great.

The Louvre article has been going a little slow, but I will have the draft to you on time. No questions yet. The Rodin Museum trip was great. The museum was actually one of the places I didn't know much about, so that made the research even more interesting.

Thanks,
Lucy Berry

## A GLIMPSE AT THE EIFFEL TOWER
### TRAVEL ARTICLE #1
#### BY LUCY BERRY | PUBLISHED SEPTEMBER 10, 2021

The Eiffel Tower, a French Monument, is the brainchild of Gustave Eiffel. Most importantly, it is a creator's dream location. A place where you can see an entire city's landscape from the top floor. I have had Paris, specifically the Eiffel Tower, at the top of my bucket list for over ten years. Finally, at the age of twenty-six, I am experiencing my first guided tour, which I highly recommend taking part in. Let's explore!

Gustave's Eiffel Tower design was almost denied when he entered his proposal into the 1889 Exposition Universelle (an event celebrating the one-hundredth anniversary of the French Revolution). On March 31, 1889, after two years, two months, and five days, workers completed the most famous landmark in Paris, France, once and for all. After one hundred thirty-two years, the tower is the heart of Paris, a wonder of the world, and my favorite place.

## FIRST FLOOR

The first floor with an illuminating glass floor was complete on April 1, 1888, creating a clear, steady platform that allows visitors to see the ground below them. I'll admit, I was a bit scared at first. I dipped my toe on the glass as my friends, and I stepped off the elevator, carefully poking at it. The view was worth my twenty seconds of fear. What seemed like millions of tourists walked below us while they looked like ants to us.

## SECOND FLOOR AND SEINE RIVER

One of the best views came when our group reached the second-floor railing. We could see the Seine River and so many French monuments such as the Louvre, Montmartre, Invalides, and Notre-Dame. As we stood there, our tour guide told us that the Seine River divides the city into two banks: the art side and the business side.

The Left Bank holds everything an artist could dream of, including Paris's early-era artists, writers, and philosophers, while the Right Bank contains all the city's rising businesses. As I gazed out at the magical cityscape, a question piqued at the back of my mind, urging me to find out where exactly one distinct location was along the Seine River.

"Is The Wall of Love on the Left Bank?" I asked my tour guide. "I assume so, but I am not sure."

"That's a great question," she said. "The Montmartre, known for The Wall of Love, is on the Left Bank and a pinnacle location for love in the neighborhood. The neighborhood itself is vibrant with art history and whimsical charm, even before the Revolution, a hub for so many artists."

A legit guided tour is worth the time and money. Take a leap of faith and join the adventure to the Eiffel Tower's summit.

## SUMMIT

There are two unique ways to reach the summit: over a thousand steps or the lift. Step by step, visitors climb 1,665 steps and 343 meters to the Eiffel Tower's summit, the final part of the greatest Parisian achievement. The alternative way to the top is to travel through the heart of the tower by boarding the lift. Either way, visitors have an insider look at the beautiful craftsmanship from another time period. Some fascinating aspects of the summit: the top floor is home to Gustave Eiffel's office, panoramic maps, the 1889 summit model, and a champagne bar.

After the two-and-a-half-hour tour, head over to the champagne bar and enjoy the view. Grab your friends, a glass, and stand at the railing on the summit. Drinking with your friends while on the Eiffel Tower is an experience that can't be missed. Take your time, explore, and enjoy everything this French monument has to offer.

*Note: Once you are in the Eiffel Tower, your ticket is one-entry only. No re-entry for the same day.*

# CHAPTER 14

# WINE CELEBRATION

———

## SEPTEMBER 10–12, 2021

We sit in a small café sipping sweet red wine from fancy wine glasses. The midday sun streams in the front windows. The bell over the entrance constantly rings as people dash in and out of the single glass door. We clink our glasses together. "Cheers!"

I take a long sip, then say, "I still can't believe I am finally published."

Jenny tips her glass to me and says, "It's happening."

Michael says, "Oh girl, your journey has only begun. You're climbing to the top." He pumps his fist in the air.

"My ultimate climb to the top. My writing journey—and my first writing position—is off to an amazing start." I take a sip of my wine and say, "Plus, I started my articles off with my favorite place in the world with my favorite people."

Jenny smiles. "Oh, you're too kind, my dear."

"She really is, isn't she?" Michael smirks.

"One of the kindest people I know."

"One of the best gals around."

An hour later, the crisp air brushes against my cheeks as we step onto the sidewalk. Everything is falling into place.

Where doubt used to easily wash over me like a layer of extra skin, now reassurance wraps its protective arms around me. I feel the wine. The city streets are narrow with cars zooming up and down them like bees in a hive. People mindlessly bustle around us while we standstill. I don't want to move. I want to take everything in, one breath at a time.

Michael shakes my shoulder and says, "You good?"

"I'm good, just taking in my surroundings and feeling good."

"That wine did get to you."

Jenny pipes up, "I believe it did."

"Well, yes. I feel at peace. I don't have doubt weighing me down." I take a deep breath.

"Are you taking Aaron's advice?"

"I am focusing on Paris and my writing; not the past." I am focusing on calming breaths and taking in all Paris has to offer.

We have so much more to see, and I am ready. My past will not hold me back any longer.

"I am so proud of you!" Jenny squeezes my arm a bit as we walk down the busy sidewalk. "Hmm, Lucy Lu, what's caught your funny bone?"

"Us walking like this, arm in arm down a sidewalk through a crowd of people, reminds me of the Sanderson Sisters from *Hocus Pocus*."

Michael says, "There you go with the movie references again."

*Hocus Pocus* makes my heart happy. I used to have it playing while I worked on homework in college. It has become a comfort movie, a script I know backward and forward. "What can I say? I love casting a good spell every now and then." I wink. I jump subjects and continue, "I can't believe I'll be turning in my second article this week."

"It feels like we just got to Paris," Jenny muses.

"It really does," Michael agrees. "Yet, we've done so much. I've written some poetry, and we've seen so much of Paris."

I gasp. "We are zooming through our Paris getaway. See what I did there?" They roll their eyes. "What? Y'all know I love my puns."

"We know," they say.

"Oh well, that's just how I roll." I smile and sway my hips to a silent beat. "Let's walk across the bridge and see where it leads us, or I can check Google?"

Jenny teases, "Okay, Mrs. Google, please check for us."

"Oh, am I married to Google now?" I throw my hand to my chest and giggle.

"You might as well be."

"Eh, it'll be a better marriage than my last one," I strongly admit.

"Lucy!"

"What? It's the truth."

They shake their heads.

"Mrs. Google has this under control! We are five minutes away from the closest mall."


We are standing in the women's section of the Le BHV Marais.

We walk over to the map. The mall has so much to offer. I scan the board for keywords that fit each of us: art, home decorating, and books. My eyes land on a book section on the second floor. I say, "Books and art supplies, next level?"

"You don't have to ask me twice," Jenny grins.

"Ditto," Michael says and skips to the escalators.

"I wonder if they sell wine here. I want some while I edit tonight." I tap my chin as I think about sipping wine and fine-tuning my article.

"If they do, we will find it just for you."

"Wine, food, and a writing session only with Lucy Berry!" Jenny says and squeezes my shoulder. We step off the escalator onto the second floor. Beautiful colors from painting supplies to books spines line the shelves. She takes a deep breath and adds, "I am in my happy place, arts of all kinds together in one place. Ah, I could spend a whole day here!"

I happily sigh. "I think we all could. I could get lost in here and be perfectly content."

Jenny says, "I don't know about y'all, but I'm going to the art supplies first. Momma needs some coloring pencils."

"Meet us over at the books shortly?" I ask.

"Yes." She pumps her fist in the air. "I'll be right back, book nerds!"

"I guess it's just you and me for a little while, Mr. Sparks." I loop my arm through his. "You ready to get lost?"

"Any day with you, Ms. Lucy Berry." He bumps my hip.

I feel like Belle from *Beauty and the Beast* as we walk up the first row. "This is what dreams are made of."

"Says the girl who has taken us in every book-related place so far on this trip. You must have a lot of dreams about books."

Jenny skips up. She has a pack of coloring pencils in one hand, and her phone held up to her ear with the other. I mouth *Who are you talking to?*

She pulls the phone away from her ear and says, "It's the hubby." She switches to speaker, and we lean closer to her phone.

I say, "Hey Aaron, are you missing your wifey?"

He says, "Lucy, you know I am. We've been talking about you."

I tilt my head. "Good things, I hope."

"Yes, all good things. Right, Jen?"

"Yes, all good things. I was telling Aaron how you are following his advice about positive thinking," Jenny says. "You know, staying focused on Paris and your writing while leaving other stuff for when we are back home."

"I am sticking to our promises, and I'm doing really good if I do say so myself."

"She is doing really good, Aaron." Michael confirms and adds, "She's stubborn, but she listens sometimes."

"Quiet but deadly. I like it," Aaron says. "I see more and more why you are good for Lucy, man. You really care about her and know she's as stubborn as they come."

My jaw drops.

"Ha! You know I understand, dude. But you're the one who's known her for like ever." He squeezes his hook on my arm.

I give him a tight grin. "Well, thanks, Sparks. You just had to agree with Aaron."

He shrugs. "I have to agree with the truth, girl."

"Listen to the man. He's a wise one," Aaron says.

"Have we created a bromance?" Jenny whispers to me.

My eyes grow wide. "Maybe. I'm not sure." I turn to Aaron and Michael. "Are y'all starting a bromance or something?"

Michael holds his hands up in surrender. "A bromance, a friendship, or just bros talking about nonsense—whatever you call what is happening here."

"Hey, hey, hey!" Aaron says, "Don't you want your two guy best friends to get along? You wanted us to talk. We hit it off before y'all left and plan to hang once y'all are back. This isn't new. Now we are just agreeing on the subject of you."

"So, it is a good thing?"

"A very good thing."

"We promise, Lucy," Michael says.

"I hate to interrupt the bromance, but I need to find wine for tonight," I exclaim.

"Yes, go get Lucy some wine," Aaron says.

Michael jumps in. "Isn't it like early in the morning for you, dude?"

"I'd be a morning person any day for my wife," Aaron gushes.

"Awe, y'all are so cute."

"Oh, stop it!" Jenny blushes.

Aaron says, "You deserve the world, babe."

I say, "Okay, y'all need a Hallmark movie, and I need wine."

"Do your research magic and get you that wine! Jenny, I love you."

"I love you, too, babe!"

Michael says, "Bye, dude!"

"Bye, Aaron, talk to you soon. I'll get on that research and fun."

"Bye Lucy and Michael. Y'all have fun, but not too much fun."


"Room service."

I smile really big. I hop off the bed and try not to fling the door open. "Good evening, ma'am. Here's your food." She rolls the cart into the room. "Where can I set the tray?"

"On the bed is fine. Thank you!" I say and point to mine and Jenny's bed.

"Food time!"

I remove the stainless steel lid, and my mouth waters. Three juicy cheeseburgers with all the fixings, seed buns gleaming with cooking oil. Huge slices of tomato practically rest more on the plate than on the patties. Mayo and ketchup ooze from the sides into a creamy puddle. Rounding out the meal are three baskets of pommes *frites*, French for fried potatoes—fat, golden, rich potato wedges with sprinkles of salt and red seasoning.

I snatch a frite and burn my fingertips.

Jenny arches her eyebrows and says, "How much wine have you already had?"

"Check my glass. I've only had a couple of sips tonight. Must be starting my buzz early." I munch on a frite.

Jenny eyes my glass on the nightstand between the beds. "Okay, fine, you pass. You are silly, Lucy Lu."

I smile and skip back over to my laptop. "I know I am, and I enjoy it so much."

"That wine must be really good, huh?" Michael teases me as he props his notebook in his lap and reaches for some food.

I smile even bigger as I type. "Oh yes, so good. Yet, my glass is all the way over there, and I'm over here at my computer."

He walks over and hands me my glass of wine. "Here's your wine, silly girl."

"Aw, thank you, Mr. Sparks. Aren't you a kind one today."

"I try to be sweet sometimes."

Jenny says, "I think he tries only for you."

I smile. "He was the only real friend I made in college, so it just makes sense. We click and get on each other's nerves. A well-balanced friendship." I turn sideways in my chair, so I can see them. "Plus, he is one of the most bluntly honest guys I know."

He looks over his glass' rim. "I most certainly am. I don't sugarcoat things."

"No, you most certainly do not. But, I'm really glad you don't. Because honestly, I would still be married to David if you hadn't told me straight up why I should divorce him."

"I wanted you to be happy. I could tell you were so stressed and upset about what he had done. I just couldn't wait around for you to come to terms with the next step. So, I do what I do best—tell you like it is. You deserve so much better, girl."

"I know I do, which is why I really am moving on from David and onto someone better." Their eyes get really big as I take a deep breath. "What? Why are y'all looking at me like that?"

Jenny bounces on the bed. "Are you going to start dating?"

Michael almost spills food on his bed. "Like moving on from David completely and finding a new boo?"

"Whoa, whoa, whoa! Slow down a bit." I hold my hands in front of me. "Maybe once we get back to Alabama, I'll start looking for someone. How about that?" Jenny and Michael both start bouncing up and down. "Goodness, y'all would think I just said y'all won the lottery or something." I shake my head and turn back to my laptop. "I didn't say dating, at least not yet. Calm down, wouldn't y'all?"

"Well, it is a big step for you. Considering you wouldn't even look at another guy when we first got to Paris."

Jenny says, "Oh, that's right. You got so mad at us that night."

I spin around and slap the back of my chair. "I know I got mad. But, in my defense, I wasn't ready yet. But now I'm ready to move on. He's moved on. I deserve to find someone as well."

Michael claps. "Yes, girl. You deserve so much better than what you got, and you are going to find it."

Jenny raises her hands. "Preach it, Sparks, preach it."

I snort. "Y'all are a hoot and a half."

## Email from Judith Garcia on September 12, 2021

Hello Ms. Berry,

I hope you and your friends are doing well and enjoying your time in Paris.

Just a quick reminder (and to have handy in our emails):

Five days from now, on September 17, your Louvre article will be posted. So, if I need any edits from you, I will email you tomorrow, September 13, through September 15, and then polish the draft and send it to our publishing team on September 16.

Rodin Museum Article due September 19, Posted on September 24.

Wall of Love Article due September 26, Posted on October 1.

I look forward to reading and editing more from you.

Best,
Judith Garcia
Editor in Chief
*Getaway Travel Magazine*

# CHAPTER 15

# WALL OF LOVE

———

## SEPTEMBER 16, 2021

The last four days have been nothing short of amazing. Jenny and Michael fill me in on the conversation we had with Aaron after too many glasses of wine the other night. Aaron was thrilled about how positive I was about my future dating life.

I remember saying that I am completely ready to move on from David. That is a conversation and revelation I will never forget, and I know Jenny and Michael will keep reminding me of it as well. Every day they mention my tipsy dating revelation, and I roll my eyes every single time.

It isn't that I don't want to date. I just don't know if a tipsy revelation is a firm foundation to start dating or not. But I know they are secretly hoping I come to my senses and listen to Tipsy Lucy. If it turns out she's right, then sober me will never live it down.

We are standing in front of The Wall of Love, which features the phrase "I love you" in over one hundred different languages. I am in absolute awe that artists would create such a loving piece of art for their community. White letters against a marble wall gleam in the morning sun. I shield my eyes to look at the phrases.

*Te quiero (Spanish), mi amas vin (Esperanto), Hondgo (Hungarian), Sayo cinta ta (Malay), Ke a go rato (Sesotho), Ti voglio bene (Italian, rather for close family and friends, than lovers), Tangiuika (Mongolian), Ndagukunda (Hindi).*

I say, "I could stay here all morning."

"We just might," Michael says.

I take a deep breath. "I hope so. Fresh air is good for the soul." People mill about around us. A lady sits on the bench in the garden area, reading a book. Kids tug at their moms' hands. The area is alive and well.

"It really is," Jenny agrees. "Especially in front of a place like this. We are in such a calming place right now."

"I know. In the middle of a beautiful garden. No better way to spend my last article research, am I right?"

"This place really shows how loving Paris can be," Michael observes.

"Isn't Paris called the City of Love?" I ponder while I stare at the wall.

"I've heard it called the City of Light and the City of Love, actually. Could it be both?" Michael tilts his head at me. "I'll google it this time."

"Yes, save me from *always* consulting Mr. Google." I clasp my hands.

"I can't make you look up everything. Sometimes I just need to do it myself."

Jenny pipes up, "We love to hear that."

I smile. "A man who takes action. We love that."

Michael waves his hand to dismiss our praises. "Oh, stop it. I just wanted to do it myself."

I put my face really close to his and say, "So, did you find anything?"

"You don't know the meaning of personal space, do you?"

I back away. "Not really, no."

He shakes his head. "Jenny, has she ever known what personal space is?"

"Ha. Lucy? Nope."

"Well, thanks for backing me up. Not." I cross my arms and huff.

She shrugs. "I can't disagree with the truth."

I know she's right, but I hate admitting it. I love hugs and being right next to people. Sometimes I get a little too close. But that's who I am. Physical touch is *my* love language.

She pats my shoulder. "What are best friends for?"

"Apparently, they are for telling the truth."

"Yes, they are." She grins really big.

Michael waves his hands between us and says, "I hate to break up this love fest, but I have an answer to our burning question." He pauses for dramatic effect. "Paris is actually both the City of Light and the City of Love. Dubbed for different reasons, but nonetheless called both phrases. How neat is that?"

I point out, "Don't they say that Paris is perfect for finding and falling in love, but also great for new ideas and arts of all kinds? The Eiffel Tower is the perfect place to find love. It's in all the movies." I roll my eyes. "Oh, to have someone propose at the top of the tower. Not that I want that or anything."

"Remember that bartender guy?" Michael wiggles his eyebrows.

"Oh lordy, not the bartender guy conversation again." I wave my hands in the air. "Why are we bringing him up? That was ages ago, y'all."

"That was the beginning of the trip."

"Yes, *ages* ago."

"No, like two weeks ago."

"Stop shaking your head at me." I put my hands on my hips. "I would much rather forget about that guy and that conversation, thank you very much."

Jenny raises her eyebrows and says, "Why, though?"

I sigh. "Because I'm not interested in finding someone in *Paris.*"

"But you're interested in finding someone back in Alabama?"

"That is a revelation that came from Tipsy Lucy," I say as bluntly as possible. "I'm not sure if Sober Lucy wants to trust her on that decision or not." I look around at the garden. "People are staring. Can we please stop?"

"Have we pushed your buttons? Because we didn't mean to do that. It was just an honest question." She starts twisting the end of her T-shirt—her nervous habit. "Maybe we should stop or go somewhere else."

"Y'all didn't push my buttons." I sigh. "I just don't want to talk about that night, okay? I didn't like fighting with y'all then, and I don't want to do it now. And I don't want to fight on if I will date in Alabama or not either. Right now, I need to move on, and I need to be okay with that step before I go searching for a new man."

Jenny bites her bottom lip and whispers, "Sorry."

I draw circles on the sidewalk with my toe as I think. I want to just be happy and carefree, but I also want to take care of my heart. I take another deep breath for good measure. "I just want to do me. If a guy comes along, cool. If it takes years, that's okay, too. I want to be okay with what's next before I break my heart by going too fast."

With sad eyes, Jenny looks at me. "We never wanted to push you. We just want you to be happy." She elbows Michael, "Don't we, Sparks?"

"Uh? Right. Yes, we do." He rubs his arm. "Sorry, I zoned out."

I shake my head and look back at the wall. All I know is that when I'm ready to date again, I'll know. I have to be patient with myself.

The day is just starting, and we are already bickering. That must be a new record or something.

Jenny breaks the silence and says, "Michael, can you consult Mr. Google to find us some restaurants to choose from around here?"

He shakes his head and types on his phone as I stare at the wall and the people around us. A few seconds later, he says, "There's a small place that way." He points to the left. "Let's go find some food." We nod our heads, and Michael leads us away from the wall.

A few blocks from the Wall of Love sits a small white building with an R on the awning. The chalkboard sign out front says, Welcome to Roberta's Italian Restaurant. A bell chimes as we open the door and cross the threshold. We order the daily specials: spaghetti, lasagna, ravioli, and a round of sweet red wine.

Michael leans across the table and says, "So are you a hundred percent positive that you don't want to at least *talk* about the subject of men right now?"

I take a long sip of my wine. They stare at me. I set my wine glass down and say, "I'm hoping to work toward dating one day. Maybe. I'm not certain."

"So what I'm hearing is Tipsy Lucy had some truth to her revelation the other night?"

"Maybe so." I am probably about to regret this conversation, but honestly, I am thinking about it. Mostly, I just want to focus on writing and exploring Paris for the next five days. I can't deny that I miss having that one central person. On the other hand, I'm not one hundred percent ready.

Jenny claps. Her flowy sleeves bounce. "I can work with 'maybe so.'"

Michael says, "What's your ideal guy?"

"Well, he has to have a good heart. A guy who will be kind to others. For example, if he's rude to the waitress or waiter on a date, then that's a 'see ya later' kind of thing."

"A woman who knows what she wants, I like it. What about looks, are those a big deal to you?"

"Not really. I like a hot guy as much as the next girl, but personality is the main thing I am attracted to, ya know?"

"Are you real?" Jenny pokes my shoulder. "Oh my gosh, that is such a wholesome answer." She turns to Michael. "Seriously, how is our Lucy still single?"

"I'm wondering that myself." He swirls the remaining wine around his glass. "Don't you want to find you a sweet guy once we are back in the States? There are so many ways to find a guy nowadays."

"Are you going to continue to push this if I decide to wait?" I ask.

"No, dating is your decision. I just want you to know that I support you. Okay?" He sets his glass down. "I know it is scary putting yourself out there. Heck, I am still single and looking for someone to mingle with, but I am not letting it keep me down, and you shouldn't either. You are smart and highly capable of being on your own, but I know you are a hopeless romantic, and I want you to be able to share that with someone."

"You want me to be happy with whatever I choose to do with my life. Right?"

"You're catching on, Ms. Berry."

"I suppose I am, Mr. Sparks. So does this mean y'all are going to help me meet someone if and when I am ready to start looking?"

"Of course, we will help you." Jenny says, "We have to protect our best girl."

"Right on, Jenny," Michael says. "We do have to protect our best girl."

"What I'm hearing is that group outings are a must." I smile.

"Oh yes!"

We come to the conclusion that maybe dating after divorce won't be so bad. As long as I have my friends to catch me when I stumble, I'll be okay. Besides, I am in the City of Light and Love. I am going to enjoy my adventure to the fullest from now on. Dating can wait.

The next morning, I rub my eyes to wake myself. The only sounds in our room are my two best friends snoring. I tiptoe over to my laptop to make some progress on my Rodin Museum article.

I am having a hard time getting it going. Research can only do so much. I am racking my brain to see what else I can talk about because I don't have enough yet. I am also starting the basic outline for my Wall of Love article.

I am one busy and stressed writer with all these deadlines.

I click on *My Jams* playlist and hit play on my favorite Jonas Brothers song. I turn the volume down and let the lyrics ease my mind. The *Back to The Future* reference makes me smile. I remember Aaron's birthday party from two years ago when all our friends dressed up as 1980s movie characters. What a fun memory. A little over a month from now, we'll be celebrating again, and I can't wait.

I sit back in the chair as the soft music fills my little bubble. My muscles start to relax. I feel a writing spark coming on and begin typing. The words flow like they have always been inside of me. Like this subject was always meant for me to write. I can do this.

Jenny sits up in bed and stretches. She yawns and says, "What time is it?"

"Almost lunchtime."

"What's for lunch?"

"Always thinking with your stomach, I see." I look over at Michael. "We can wait to wake him because I kind of want to get room service for lunch."

"Do you want to keep writing and waiting for your second article to post, by chance?"

"Ah, you know me so well, Jen."

"I do what I can." She waves her hand and bows. "When is your article posting?"

I prop my elbows on the back of my chair and rest my chin on my hands. "Hopefully, I will get an email from my editor in the next hour and a half. Around two o'clock."

"You have time to eat some yummy food and write some more. Then, we can celebrate by watching the sunset at the Eiffel Tower since we didn't stay out late last night for your last article day. I can't believe you forgot."

"Hey, we *all* forgot."

"All right, you have me there." She reaches over to the hotel phone on the nightstand and dials room service. Michael stirs, then opens one eye, checking to see what is going on before rolling over on his stomach and snoring into his pillow. I shake my head. She hangs up the phone and says, "Our food and drinks are ordered."

In four days, we will be boarding a plane back to Alabama. Part of me wants to get back home to see my family, and the other part wants to stay in Paris forever. I love my new writing position because who knows where they will have me travel for my next assignment? My wish list includes London, Ireland, or Rome for my future writing adventures. I want to see Big Ben in person. Now, that would be fascinating. Loud knocking breaks me out of my travel daydream.

"Room service."

I skip over to the foot of Michael's bed and stare at him. I whisper, "Time to rise and shine, Master of the Darkness. Food's here. Wake up, Sparks." He rustles the covers as I grab my buzzing phone from the nightstand.

# CHAPTER 16

# SECOND TRAVEL ARTICLE

———

## SEPTEMBER 17, 2021

Hello Ms. Berry,

I hope this email finds you and your friends doing well! Your Louvre article is live on our website! You are now free to post and share wherever you'd like. https://www.getawaytravelmag.com/louvre

Excellent job on this piece! I look forward to reading your Rodin article, which is due in two days. Then, your last article, "The Wall of Love," is due the following week. Keep up the great work, Ms. Berry.

Best,
Judith Garcia
Editor in Chief
*Getaway Travel Magazine*

## A TRIP TO THE LOUVRE
### TRAVEL ARTICLE #2
### BY LUCY BERRY | PUBLISHED SEPTEMBER 17, 2021

The Louvre Museum is the world's largest museum and a historic monument in Paris. The remarkable property resides on the Seine River's Right Bank. The location is the city's first arrondissement, which is a subdivision of a French department for the local government administration.

One of the featured pieces is Leonardo da Vinci's famous painting, the *Mona Lisa*. Sealed and protected behind a bulletproof case, the enchanting art remains in prime condition after over five hundred years. Visitors can find the beautiful woman in the Louvre's largest room along with Veronese's painting, *The Wedding Feast at Cana*. I highly recommend spending a few hours gazing at the legendary artists.

### HISTORY

Before the building became a museum, it was a fortress (military stronghold), built in 1190 then reconstructed in the sixteenth century to a glorious royal palace. For two centuries, the Louvre remained a royal palace before becoming a museum in 1793, gaining a collection of five hundred thirty-seven paintings. The opening was short-lived as it closed in 1796 due to structural problems. Five years later, Napoleon reopened the museum and expanded the collection by thousands of donated artworks from all over the world. He renamed the museum after himself after setting the foundation for the Louvre's presence in the art community. For over ten years, Napoleon made a difference in the museum's future, but it didn't last. After almost five thousand artworks were returned to their countries after Napoleon was stripped of his powers with the Treaty of Fontainebleau, the Louvre reverted back to its original name. The collection continued to expand and flourish into the Louvre that we know and love today.

## MONA LISA

The painting's reputation holds true. The piece took sixteen years to complete and spans generations of art education. In 1911, The Mona Lisa acquired a set of guards after being stolen from the museum and not recovered until 1913, when a former employee tried to sell the beloved piece. Since 1913, the famous lady has been kept in a bulletproof glass case to keep anyone from snatching the gem again.

The glass is illuminated by its own LED lamp. A wooden railing protects the case from fingerprints. Held by an oak frame, the woman is magnificent and enchanting. She looks into the distance, almost feeling like she is staring at the audience, pulling them into her surroundings. The backdrop is faded, a mountain view with rolling hills, ridged canyons, and forest pines against a blue and yellow sky. From the distant look in her eyes to the wrinkles in her sleeves, Leonardo made her lifelike. She resembles a brave and gentle wealthy girl searching for more in this world. A woman with the world at her fingertips and a wonder of the world.

Although the Louvre has far more to offer visitors than just the Mona Lisa, I highly recommend spending a portion of your visit studying Leonardo's masterpiece. I believe that art can speak to us more than we give it credit for, so embrace the unknown and learn more about what makes this painting famous.

# CHAPTER 17

# THE FINAL ADVENTURE

———

## SEPTEMBER 17–18, 2021

The evening sun is casting a soft glow behind the Eiffel Tower as the day slowly shifts to night. I sit on the lawn surrounded by tourists and locals alike. I am savoring every last breath of Paris on our final week. I pour us each a small glass of sweet red wine. Reclining on one elbow, I casually take a sip. I feel at ease while we wait for the tower to light the city once again. The iron gleams against the pitch-black sky. The tower is the brightest place in Paris, a beacon that brings people home. A tiny star leading travelers to discover the city's wonders.

I exclaim, "How are we already on the last week?"

"I honestly don't know where the time went," Jenny says, "One minute we stepped off the plane, the next we are sipping wine on one of our last nights."

Michael says, "I am going to miss waking up in Paris." He bumps my shoulder.

My wine swirls in my glass. "Sleeping until *noon*, that is."

"Sometimes you just have to sleep until noon when you are on vacation, okay?"

"Well, at least you waited until the final week." I bump his shoulder.

"No better time to do it, I'll say." Jenny gasps. "I still can't believe you took me to *Paris. Paris!* It feels like that first phone call was yesterday. You really are making your dreams come true, Lucy, and I am so glad I can be a small part of your journey." She fans her face. "Oh, I am going to make myself tear up."

"Stop it. You are going to make *me* tear up!" I quickly wipe the tears from my eyes.

"I think we need to head back to the hotel before we are a puddle of tears." She shifts to her knees and slips her phone in her back pocket.

"We can continue this gush fest in the room."

Michael says, "Only you would call it a gush fest."

"It just fits my personality." I wink and slip my phone into my purse.

We roll up our throw blanket and gather up our wine and glasses. We make our short walk to Cler Hotel. I am going to miss this walk so much.

The twinkling lights and stars make me want to stay forever. I wouldn't mind coming back. Whether it be for a writing assignment or a getaway trip with someone special, I know I could always be happy here. My doubts and worries melt away when I walk around this beautiful city, and I hope I always strive to be just like this wherever life takes me next.

I unlock the hotel room door and immediately pour myself some more wine. Tonight is about relaxing, laughing, and having fun. Our last week all in the same room and city.

After a few glasses of wine and a call from Aaron, my eyes are stinging. I plug my phone in, adjust the comforter, and turn the lamp off. "Goodnight, silly best friends. I love y'all." I suddenly feel my eyes start to flutter as my body goes into a deep sleep.


I scream at the man standing in front of me. "I don't love you anymore!"

"Why am I here?" David squints and studies my body language and facial expressions.

I cross my arms and shrug. "I had too much wine. I'm exhausted. The return trip to Alabama is inching closer and closer."

"Hitting wine too hard? Gracious, Lucy." He taps his foot against the hardwood floors.

We are in *my* house, but it looks like it did when we were married, right down to the Christmas tree in the corner of the room. I twist my ring and notice I am wearing my wedding band.

"Why are we back at Christmas? What year is it?"

He points at the calendar dangling from a hook on the wall. "It is the week of Christmas 2019, Luce. We are happily married."

My heart is beating super fast. "I remember how happy we were. Emphasize on the *were!* We can't be like that ever again! You ruined that for us. You chose *her!*" I jerk my body away from him. He isn't mine. He is hers. I am meant for someone else.

"We can be happy together," he says. "I'll leave her, I promise. My heart belongs to you and only you. You are my sweetheart."

"We will *never* be happy together ever again! Get out of my head. You aren't wanted here!"

He vanishes, and I am left alone, standing in the middle of what used to be our living room. I stare at the tree and wonder how something so magical could exist in a loveless home. A home where cheating, yelling, and fighting happened in the middle of 2020 that ultimately tore us apart for good.

"Lucy, wake up! Lucy, time to wake up. You need to do some writing." The twinkling lights on the Christmas tree become brighter and brighter as the voice comes closer and closer.

"What time is it?" I rub my eyes and look up into Jenny's eyes.

She scrunches up her nose and says, "Early in the morning. Are you okay?"

"David was in my dream again," I groan, and she stares at me. "Yes, I'm over him. I had too much wine and had been up way too long. It's fine. I'm fine."

"Okay, I was just checking." Her voice catches, and my heart breaks.

I shouldn't have been so rude. I take a deep breath and clear my thoughts. "I'm sorry. That came out ruder than I expected it to." The lump in my throat bobbles.

She wipes her face. "It's okay. That dream must have been very shocking and confusing."

Michael pats my foot and says, "We just want to make sure you're okay, girl."

My heart melts. "I know. I know. I'm just frustrated. He shouldn't have been in my dream, that's all."

Jenny squeezes my shoulder. "You are so right. He shouldn't have. Your mind is playing tricks on you, and you don't deserve that nonsense!"

"You really don't! Like I said last year, you deserve better than him," Michael says. "You deserve someone who will love you and tell you the truth always. Okay? And I know you'll find that someday."

"I don't deserve y'all." I pull them into a hug. "Thank you for loving me through everything."

"No matter what you face in life, I'll be here for you, Lucy Lu." Jenny chokes up and presses her face into my shoulder. Michael exclaims, "I second that!" They squeeze me tighter. "To ease your mind, we are heading to the park in a little bit."

"I can't believe it is our last Saturday in Paris!" We step onto the curb. Jenny and I follow Michael to the grassy area adjacent to the Corinthian Colinnacle, which is the long sequence of columns that border the Parc Monceau's pond and garden area. A gentle breeze rustles the few trees around us. Joggers in athletic attire and Bluetooth headphones run past us on the sidewalk. Two German shepherds with their tongues happily hanging out lead their dog walker. A group of college students surrounded by books are laughing near the edge of the pond.

We spread our blanket on the ground. I open my laptop bag, carefully removing the items and setting them in front of me, my laptop, notebook, and a variety of pens and pencils. Jenny has her sketchpad on her knees and is staring into the distance. Michael slowly runs his pen across his spiral-bound notebook

"I'm not ready to leave," Jenny says, "There's no better spot to draw. This scenery is perfect, an artist's dream location."

"I agree," I say. "This is one of the most perfect cities in the world to create art in."

"Some of the best artists came from here."

"This place is so inspirational. I didn't just pick these article topics for their rich history, but also the inspiration they bring to my writing."

Michael says, "Plus, the off-topic locations you picked are amazing and spooky." He props his black spiral-bound notebook on his knee. "The columns over there, what if ghost children were running in between them? They could be playing hide-and-seek and giggling."

"I see what you did there." I close my eyes and picture the scene. "It reminds me of the ending of *Hocus Pocus*. Oh, Emily and Binx, I love that movie."

Jenny says, "That movie is timeless."

"How can you not love the Sanderson Sisters?"

"The baddest witches in Salem." Jenny laughs, then turns to Michael. "How is your writing coming, Sparks?" She lightly sketches as she talks. I wonder if she is drawing the greenery or the architecture around us.

"I have ideas. They just aren't coming out on paper." His shoulders slump. "I want to write and publish horror poetry, but my publishing dream is looking far off."

Jenny slams her pencil down. "No dream is ever too far off. Only quitters say that, and I don't see you as a quitter, Michael Sparks! Or should I say Mr. Spook Master Sparks? Because you were born to be spooky, okay? What's your middle name? Because I need to use it now."

His eyes get really big. He whispers, "James."

"Michael James Sparks, you are the Spook Master. You are the King of Darkness in this friend group. You are the night to Lucy's day. You are incredibly brilliant, and don't you dare think any different, sir." She puts her hands on her hips and stares at him.

"I hear you loud and clear. Wow, you know how to give a prep talk and scare a little bit." He gives her a loud round of applause.

"Thank you, thank you."

He smiles. "I guess I better get writing, huh?"

"Yes, because one day your name is going to be known everywhere."

"Yes, ma'am."

I say, "Ah, I love this energy."

Jenny says as she sketches, "How's *your* writing going?"

"It is actually going really well. Want to hear some of it?"

"Always!"

Michael's head pops up. "Read, girl!"

"Okay, so this is the first few sentences from the section on *The Thinker*. Remember, this is only a rough draft."

*As a poet, I am intrigued at how The Thinker and The Gates of Hell sculptures came to be a reality for Rodin. It truly speaks to the notion that artists are inspired by each other and different art forms. In 1880, Auguste Rodin was inspired by Dante's poem about Hell, Divine Comedy. Very spooky to create something so terrifying to be perceived as art, yet it turned out remarkable.*

"I love the spooky part," Michael says, "Rough drafts can still be magical!"

"I knew you would, seeing how we did some improv with these sculptures." I shrug. "I'm pretty magical."

"That was a fun day." He smirks.

"One of the best. Now to crank out an awesome article to match." After a beat, I add, "I don't have to think about deadlines until next week when we are back in Alabama. We can relax tomorrow before we spend the next day packing."

Jenny frowns. "When you put it that way, it makes me sad that we have to leave so soon. I miss my hubby, but I love Paris so much."

"I bet you miss your hubby." I nudge her.

Jenny waves her hand. "Hmm, maybe a little."

I bite my bottom lip as my thoughts run away from me. I spill out, "Well, I hate to cut this exciting moment short, but I need to know if this article is finished or not. Help me!" Sweat beads run down my face.

*Why am I suddenly so stressed? Second to last article, last one before we leave Paris. It will be okay.*

Jenny says, "Lucy Lu, take a few deep breaths. It is okay. You are in the fresh air, deep breaths. Happy thoughts only."

I breathe in and out. "Okay. I'm okay. I'm okay now. I am magical!"

Michael shifts closer to me and slowly rubs circles on the small of my back. He says, "You will get it done. I'll get your laptop and look at your article, okay? You just lie down on the blanket and close your eyes." I lie down. Michael's typing and Jenny's whispering fade as I escape into my dream world.

Michael shakes my shoulders and gently talks to me. I open my eyes. "There you go," he says and hands my laptop back to me. "Go submit that article, girl."

The warm sun pings off my screen. I shield my eyes as I slowly wake up. I turn the brightness up and get to work.

Good afternoon,

I hope this email finds you doing well.

Here is my Rodin Museum article submission.

I have started the outline for my fourth and final Paris article, "The Wall of Love." There isn't much to put into the article. I am thinking about adding a conversation I had with my best friends about how Paris is called both the City of Love and the City of Light. It seems like a fun debate. Leaving for Alabama soon.

I look forward to hearing from you.

Thanks,
Lucy Berry

Hello Ms. Berry,

I am doing well! It sounds like you are thrilled to be on the last leg of your Paris trip but also sad to see it end. But no worries, there will be more adventures in the future. We can talk about future plans later on, but for now, I will tell you that we want to start a local section for our writers and readers as well by sending our writers to in/out-of-state locations for adventures closer to home. You will travel within Alabama and the United States at least through New Year's Day. On that note, you will also have a month off once you are home (September 22–October 22) to rest and recharge.

I look forward to reading your work. I can't wait to see how you articulate the debate in your piece.

Do you have your travel squared away?

I know that was a lot of information, so don't hesitate to ask questions. Hope to hear from you soon.

Thank you for being on top of deadlines through this process.

Best Wishes,
Judith Garcia
Editor in Chief
*Getaway Travel Magazine*


Hello,

All of that sounds very exciting.

I am so glad you think it is a good idea. Yes, we have all of our flight information on my phone.

I am glad I can help make things run smoother like you have done for me through this process. I was so nervous coming into this new position, but you have made the experience so great. I can't wait for more.

Talk soon,
Lucy Berry

# CHAPTER 18

# SAYING GOODBYE

———

## SEPTEMBER 20–21, 2021

Two days later, after spending the morning packing and sipping wine, we are in a small café around the corner from the Eiffel Tower.

I am dreading leaving Paris.

Tomorrow we will board our flight home, and I still can't believe it. It feels like yesterday that we checked into our hotel and started exploring the city, but that was weeks ago. I stare out the window at the busy sidewalks and streets. People are everywhere, running around under the soft glow of the afternoon sun. Another hour comes and goes. We eat until our bellies are full and our eyes are heavy. Sluggish and dreading the flight home, I am not ready.

As sunset draws closer, I become more and more sentimental about our time in Paris. There wasn't enough, but I'll be back one day. I can hold on to that dream. My first article series location assignment is almost over. I have only a few more hours in the city that captured my heart when I was a kid. I have lived my biggest dream, and I can't wait to live more through this position. *Getaway Travel Magazine's* website promises adventure—every girl's dream job. I plan to take as many adventures as possible.

We walk by the Eiffel Tower, and I come to a sudden halt. I take in the fresh evening air. "Ah, that Paris air, there's nothing like it in the whole wide world."

Michael teases me, "Are you high on something or what?"

"High on life, yes. High on something else? Absolutely not. Who do you think I am?"

"Man, do I love teasing you. It reminds me of college writing sessions late at night."

Jenny says, "Writing sessions late at night?"

"We would stay up all night writing to meet deadlines. Well, for me too. Lucy was always ahead. She is rather impressive."

"Impressive?" I grin. "Me? No, I'm not impressive at all. I am just little old me."

"You really are, girl." He shoves my shoulder. "I promise I will never lie about that."

"My determination is who I am, and I am glad that impresses you." I strut and look over my shoulder at them.

Jenny whistles and claps for me. "Looking good, Lucy Lu!"

Only she would whistle for me in the middle of a crowded sidewalk. I throw my head back and laugh. I finally feel so happy after stressing so much the last few days. The stress bubbles are still there, but they are much more manageable.

Jenny says, "Someone seems happier. No more worries?"

"I'll worry about it when we board the plane." I spread my arms out and happily skip. "I feel like I am floating on air."

*I will shove my worries to the backburner. I am going to enjoy our last few hours here. I will not force it. I will let the happiness overtake me.*

The light breeze blows my hair around my face. I can't wait to sit in front of the Eiffel Tower and watch the sunset on our final night here. I hold my stomach as I catch my breath. "We should get macaroons. One last memory in this beautiful city."

Jenny agrees, "No better way to end our trip than with macaroons and the Eiffel Tower sunset. Kind of like a send-off party, maybe?"

"You understand my brain, Jen." I bounce up and down on my tiptoes.

"Well, I am your best friend, Lucy Lu."

"You at least understand it enough to communicate with me and understand my ideas. That is definitely a major plus."

"It really is, my dear. Now let's go get those macaroons before the sun sets without us."

"The sun isn't allowed to set without us," Michael says, grabbing our arms. He drags us along the sidewalks until we are at the macaroon shop.

We munch on our treats as we spread our blanket on the lawn. The soft glow of the sunset beams behind the beautiful Eiffel Tower. Another perfect end to an amazing day. I could stay here forever, but I know it is time to return home. My family is waiting, and I can't wait to see them.

Paris calls my name, but Alabama is where I call home.

Michael smiles and says, "This is the best sunset of the trip." The sky changes colors as it slowly makes its way to pitch-black. The perfect backdrop for the highlight attraction. "One last selfie before the sky completely changes to nighttime, gals?"

I giggle and say, "Did you even have to ask?" I can't wait to relive the magic through our photos.

Jenny says, "We gals love making photo memories!"

"Say Paris on three. One... two... three." Michael steadies his phone. "Paris," we say together as the sky changes to orange tones and slightly darkens. I smile as the sky paints beautiful strokes across the horizon. "Should I go ahead and post it on my Instagram? And text it to y'all, of course."

"The first posting of many." I cheer. "Let's give everyone a little taste of our magical adventure."

My phone buzzes with an Instagram notification from his account: @sparkshorrors tagged you in a post. We are smiling really big with a magical Paris backdrop. The caption reads: When in Paris, September 20, 2021.

I say, "Oh, Michael, you used my phrase."

"Of course. I think it is adorable."

"The most adorable phrase ever. Time to go back to the room." The lights twinkle on the Eiffel Tower, and people start moving around us. We walk back to our hotel. Five fifteen is going to come bright and early tomorrow.

I don't want to leave, not yet, but it is time.

I roll over, grab my phone, and shut off my alarm. Jenny stretches with her eyes slightly open. Michael groans as he notices us staring at him. I yell, "It's five-thirty. We need to be ready to catch a taxi in thirty minutes."

Michael whines. "It is too early to yell." He throws his extra pillow and hits me square in the face.

"Ow! Do you mind?"

"I wanted you to stop yelling."

"Well, all you had to do was ask me to stop." I sit up and cross my arms. I frown at him. I would have much rather been hit with Cupid's arrow over that pillow any day, and that's saying a lot. Maybe I am ready, or maybe I am just irritated. Either way, I could have done without the pillow throwing this morning. "I'm sorry I yelled. We need to get up, that's all."

"I forgive you." He shuffles to the bathroom.

Twenty minutes later, we slide into our taxi. I look out the window. Goodbye to walking by the Eiffel Tower and the café around the corner. Goodbye to all the shopping locations and bookstores that I love so much. I prop my elbow on the window. I am going to miss ending the night at the Eiffel Tower and waking up next to my best friends. I am going to miss so many things.

The taxi stops in front of the airport. We pay and merge into the hustle and bustle of the morning rush. After finding our gate, we make a beeline for food.

Jenny says, "Are you feeling better about leaving Paris, Lucy Lu?"

"Eh, kind of. I have accepted that Alabama is my home, not Paris. It is a process, but I am getting there."

"Slowly but surely." She abruptly comes to a halt in front of the only open restaurant at this end of the airport. The bacon smell hits my nostrils. My mouth waters as I inch closer to the menu. I walk to the counter to order for all of us.

The employee says, "Welcome to Sunny's Corner, where we serve hot breakfast all day long. I'm Lilly. How may I help you?"

"I'll have one biscuit and a side of gravy with scrambled eggs, then a chicken biscuit, and lastly a sausage biscuit with a side of hash brown. Three medium Cokes."

We slide into a booth close to the counter, and I say, "I am going to take such a good nap on the plane after I eat all of this food!"

Michael shakes his head. "I swear, all that goes on in your brain is writing, food, and sleep."

"I'm a catch." I flip my hair.

"I'm happy to be friends with such an amazing woman like yourself."

Jenny says, "He's not wrong, even if he's trying to butter you up, Lucy Lu."

"I drive all the men crazy," I joke. "They can bring their milkshakes to my yard at any time." A waiter sets our food on the table, and we move right along to the next topic. "When do y'all think we should let our parents know we are heading home?"

Jenny says, "I would probably wait until we land in North Carolina. By then, it'll be a decent time. Later, we can call them when we board our last flight."

Michael says, "If I call my parents before seven in the morning, they'll think something is wrong."

"If I wasn't already awake at six-thirty, I would not want a phone call waking me up," I bluntly state. "I feel like I would be so mean if that ever happens, like the Grinch during Christmas, I suppose."

Jenny laughs. "You are only happy on a holiday or vacation early morning."

"I do love my sleep, and I hate for it to be interrupted by anyone other than myself."

She rolls her eyes. "Hate is an understatement, but okay."

We finish our breakfast and walk to our gate. I gaze out the huge panel windows as planes leave the runaway. As I am daydreaming about napping on the plane, the crackling speaker interrupts my thoughts. The flight attendant says over the intercom, "Flight to Barcelona is now boarding. Flight 110 is now boarding. Please proceed to the loading entrance now. Have your ticket ready."

We scan our tickets and walk down the ramp into the plane's door. I happily bounce to row five and slide next to the window. I sit down and put my carry-on in my lap. I dig my headphones out while Jenny and Michael sit down beside me. The seatbelt light comes on, and a flight attendant walks up and down the aisle to make sure everyone is buckled in okay. The pilot announces, "We are ready for takeoff! Thank you for choosing American Express Airlines." The plane rumbles underneath us.

Jenny teases me, "Naptime for Lucy."

Michael reassures me, "Don't let her bother you, girl. Napping is amazing."

I roll my eyes. "Well, whatever it is, I'll see y'all when we land. Night." I put my headphones in and fall into a deep sleep.

Music is playing somewhere, just a few beats here and there. I can't make out the lyrics. Barely above a whisper, a mysterious voice says, *Lucy, Lucy, time to get off the plane. Are you okay? Lucy?"*

"I'm awake. I'm awake. I promise." I put my hands in front of me. "Back away from me, please."

Jenny says, "Grab your carry-on and follow us, okay?"

I yawn. "Got it. Following."

Another stress dream, another version of him in my head. I push the thoughts away as I scramble to keep up with Jenny and Michael. We exit the plane into the hustle and bustle of the Barcelona airport. I barely hear Jenny say, "We have a two to three-hour layover until we board our second flight."

We pass through crowds upon crowds of travelers as we make our way to our gate. I think we are somewhere in the middle. I look up at the number signs and see that they are in descending order. Ours should be coming up. Finally, after pushing through a family of twelve, I see our gate number. Good ole eighty-five reigns again. I make a beeline to the first row of empty seats. They are by the window, perfect for watching airplanes come and go. The day is clear and bright even though it isn't even noon yet. A few airplanes are on the runway with employees directing them.

Michael says, "Go watch your airplanes, silly girl." He shakes his head. I look to Jenny for her confirmation. She just smiles and nods toward the big glass-panel windows. I happily skip away from them and sit cross-legged on the floor. I settle into a plane watching daze as the minutes until boarding quickly tick by. I watch plane after plane take off into the sky, still as amazed as I was as a little girl.

# CHAPTER 19

# HELLO AMERICA

———

## SEPTEMBER 21, 2021

We are almost home. I pull out my phone and start a new text message in my *Parents* group chat. I signal to Jenny and Michael to do the same. All the time zones confuse me, but somehow I manage to send a decent message. Soon enough, I'll be able to hug my parents. I've missed them so much.

*Parents Group Chat*

Me: We made it to North Carolina. We board our flight to Huntsville at 10:30 p.m. (9:30 p.m.). We'll land at 10:53 p.m. at Gate 85. I love y'all, and I'll see y'all tonight. Jenny is staying the night with me, and Aaron is coming over tomorrow. No worries about getting her home tonight.

"I texted my parents," I say. "Aaron has to work the night shift tonight, right?" I bite my lip.

"Yeah, he is." She rolls her eyes. "No one would take the shift."

"On a scale from one to ten, how pissed are you?" If she could give Aaron's coworkers an earful, I bet a hundred bucks she would in a heartbeat.

"A solid twenty. It is just a clerk position. Why couldn't someone be kind enough to switch with him? I want to see my hubby." She crosses her arms and pouts.

"You will, Jen. You will." I rub her shoulder. "It'll just be tomorrow morning. He'll be off for what, two days?" I try to be positive. I know how much she wants to hug and kiss Aaron, but work can't be helped when coworkers won't step up.

She perks up a bit. "He will be. Thanks, Lucy Lu. I'm glad I won't be alone tonight."

Michael says, "Y'all are adorable." He types on his phone.

"Aw, thank you, boi." I smile.


Many hours later, the flight attendant scans my ticket's barcode and motions me through to the loading door. We board our final flight. I am so ready to sleep in my own bed. I lay my head on Michael's shoulder. "I am so happy to be flying home now."

He pats the top of my head and says, "I will only ever allow you to do this because it is so dang cute." We are preparing each other for future romantic relationships. I couldn't imagine doing that for anyone else.

"Y'all are absolutely precious," Jenny says and snaps a photo of us. "I just have to save this memory forever."

"Always have been, always will be. Right, Sparks?"

Michael says, "With you? Forever and always, Lucy." With happy visions in my head, I fall into a deep sleep. The plane rumbles underneath me.

"Lucy, hi. Lucy, we are in Huntsville." I rub my eyes and look out the window to a pitch-black night sky. We are back home. Jenny and Michael are staring at me. I gather my carry-on, phone, and earphones and follow them down the aisle.

A few minutes later, we merged into the busy airport in search of our luggage and my parents. A lot of people are milling about the walkways for a Tuesday night at nearly eleven o'clock. I turn my head from side to side as I say, "I'm going to let my parents know that we will meet at the luggage return."

Me: We are on our way to the luggage return. Meet y'all there?

Mom: We can meet you in twenty minutes. We just parked.

Dad: We shouldn't be too long. I know this airport like the back of my hand, ha.

Me: Yes, all your traveling is coming in handy. Definitely shaking my head at you now!

Dad: Shake your head all you want. It is the best thing to know my way around.

Me: No more getting lost.

Mom: Your dad was the worst about getting lost in the airport.

Me: Must be where I get it from.

Mom: It is. We will see you soon, sweetheart.

Me: See you soon.

"We are all set, y'all." I look up to see more signs for the luggage return. "We will not get lost. If we do, I will never live it down."

Fifteen minutes later, I scanned the luggage return area for my parents. Their hints of gray hair make them look closer to their age after all these years. Even with a twenty-six-year-old daughter, they still resemble young adults in love, with their bright eyes and shiny brunette locks. My mom's brunette and gray curls bob above the crowd. I finally reach them. Their faces light up, and they open their arms. We embrace into a tight group hug. My mom says, "Oh honey, we are so happy that you are home. We've missed you so much." She kisses the top of my head.

"I missed you both so much, too. Sorry we didn't talk as much as normal. I can't wait to tell y'all everything about the trip. Oh, y'all haven't met Michael yet!"

They release me. My dad says, "That's okay. We can now."

"We are very eager to, sweetheart," my mom says as Jenny and Michael walk up.

I smile at them. "Welcome to the party, y'all. Sorry that I kind of skipped off."

Michael shakes his head. "We knew you would, silly girl." He turns to my parents and sticks out his hand. He says, "Hello, Mr. and Mrs. Berry, I'm Michael Sparks. It is nice to officially meet you."

My dad shakes his hand and says, "I'm Mr. Alexander Berry. It is nice to officially meet you as well, Michael."

My mom follows his lead and shakes Michael's hand. "And I'm Mrs. Lindsay Berry. I'm so glad we get to finally meet you, Michael. Thank you for taking care of our girl."

Michael blushes. "I'm glad Lucy asked me to go. I'll always protect her."

I throw my arms around his neck. "Aw, boi, I love you so much."

"I love you more, girl."

Jenny says, "Okay, aw, I want in on this."

I am going to miss random group hugs every day. "As much as I love hugging y'all, I am ready to go home. Well, Jenny will be coming home with me for now, but it is basically her second home."

Michael confesses, "As much as I don't want to leave y'all, I am ready to sleep in my own bed."

Jenny says, "I mean, I have one more night of Lucy Lu, so I'm ready whenever we are ready to say bye for now to Sparks."

"Sparks, you are a hard one to part with, but," I hold up my pointer finger, "we will see you soon."

We hug and say our goodbyes to Michael as he walks to a different part of the parking deck. Jenny and I stick to my parents as they navigate the way to their car. The twisting and turning is making me grateful they came and picked up my car so we wouldn't have to remember where we parked. I make a mental note to ask Michael to let us know when he is home.

After many turns, we make it to my parents' charcoal-black Nissan Versa. My dad unlocks the vehicle, and I open the back hatch. I lift mine and Jenny's suitcases into the back and then shut the door. I slap my hands together. "All right, time to head home."

An hour later, we turned into my driveway.

Home sweet home.

I fling open my door as soon as my dad puts the car in park. I slam my feet on the ground and take in the view. I am finally back at my little home. No matter where I jet off to, this will always be my landing place. My phone buzzes in my pocket.

*Besties Group Chat*

Michael: My parents say hi. My cats are happy to have me home.

Me: You beat me to texting you. Glad you made it home. We just parked at my house.

Jenny: Even though I am standing right next to Lucy, I'll answer too. Glad you made it home, Sparks.

Michael: Aw, you are more than welcome to text, Jen, even though you aren't technically home yet.

Me: Oh, this is her second home. I kidnap her anytime I need company or Aaron is working the night shift.

Michael: You love your Jenny time.

Me: We just make sense.

Michael: I am so thankful to be included now.

Jenny: You'll forever be included. We love you, Sparks.

Michael: I love y'all, too.

Jenny: This trio is forever, dude.

Me: Ugh, I am still gushing over y'all. I am heading inside to get ready for bed. Too many hours of flying, y'all, and not enough sleep.

Jenny: Says the girl who slept most of today.

Michael: How are you sleepy?

Me: I just am. Jenny is standing right beside me as I yawn. Ask her.

Jenny: She is yawning. I'll make sure she doesn't trip over her own two feet.

Michael: Glad she has you.

Jenny: Me too.

We wave at my parents as they back out of my driveway. Their car lights bounce off the garage and onto the mailbox. I unlock the door and push into my foyer. Dropping my keys on the table, I roll my suitcase to my bedroom. Jenny clicks the door shut and turns the lock. She pads down the hall after me. I yell from my bedroom, "Have you texted Aaron yet?"

She rounds the corner and says, "You didn't have to yell. I was almost in your room. Yes, I texted him. He said hi. We already said goodnight." She twirls a piece of hair around her finger.

I rummage through my dresser and find a pair of soft pajama pants. I pair them with a comfy graphic tee and fuzzy socks. "Aw, he's so sweet. Time for bed." I bounce onto my bed and pat the comforter beside me, "Pajamas and bed, bestie."

She rolls her eyes. Fluffy pajama pants, graphic tee, and fuzzy socks to match. We really are best friends. She says, "Is this better, Lucy Lu?"

I bounce onto my knees. "Yes."

I set my alarm for ten. I turn on my *Jams* playlist, so we have sound in the house. I snuggle under the covers and fall asleep.

# CHAPTER 20

# THIRD TRAVEL ARTICLE

———

## SEPTEMBER 24, 2021

Hello Ms. Berry,

I hope this email finds you well and settling back into home life.

It has been a pleasure watching your writing grow while working with you. Thank you for editing and making the process so enjoyable.

Next month, I will send you your upcoming article topics so you can prepare. Until then, rest up and live life. You've earned it.

Your third article is published!

Link: https://www.getawaytravelmag.com/rodin-museum

One last reminder: The Wall of Love article is due very soon, and I look forward to reading it.

Take care and talk soon,

Judith Garcia
Editor in Chief
*Getaway Travel Magazine*

## RODIN MUSEUM
### TRAVEL ARTICLE #3
#### BY LUCY BERRY | PUBLISHED SEPTEMBER 24, 2021

The Rodin Museum, dating back to 1919, is primarily dedicated to Auguste Rodin's artwork. The Hotel Biron grounds are beautiful, with the lushest greenery and wide sidewalks that lead visitors to the mansion-like building. To capture the old-style feel the structure is complete with tower endcaps and long, oval-shaped windows. The property features an incredible garden that houses some of Rodin's most notable art pieces, such as *The Gates of Hell* and *The Thinker*.

Auguste Rodin was born in Paris on November 12, 1840. His most famous work didn't come until he was forty. During his forties until the end of his life in 1917, he worked on his sculpture, *The Gates of Hell*, which resides in the gardens of the Rodin Museum. Like most artists, he didn't have the easiest start to his career. While pursuing his love for crafting sculptures, he received multiple rejections in the early years.

Finally, after many years of hardship, the Salon in Paris accepted his original piece, *The Age of Bronze*, in 1877. Although this isn't one of his well-known sculptures, this is the sculpture that broke ground in his budding art career. Three years later, the Museum of Decorative Art commissioned him to create his most famous bronze door sculpture, *The Gates of Hell*. Even though this piece wasn't finished at the time of his passing, the sculpture inspired many other pieces, including his most famous one, *The Thinker*.

Despite his slow rise to fame, critics consider Rodin one of the greatest portraitists in the history of sculpture because he dabbled in bronze and marble figures during his lifetime. One of his most popular sculptures includes *The Thinker*, which appears in Ben Stiller's movie, *Night at the Museum: Battle of the Smithsonian*. This is how I first heard of his sculpture. My prior knowledge of *The Thinker* led me down a research rabbit hole. *The Thinker* and a few other sculptures were once just small sculptures on a bronze door called *The Gates of Hell*, which showcases two hundred figures. The massive bronze door was inspired by Dante's *Divine Comedy*, a poem about Hell.

As a poet, I find that *The Thinker* and *The Gates of Hell* sculptures truly speak to the notion that artists are inspired by each other and different art forms. *Divine Comedy* is a terrifying poem that provokes creativity and self-reflection. *The Thinker*, a man deep in thought, represents the biggest part of Rodin's inspiration by breaking the fourth wall. The piece directly speaks to the audience. Before donning the popular name of *The Thinker*, Rodin originally called his bronze masterpiece *The Poet*.

Not only did he include elements from the circles of Hell, but Rodin also incorporated the man himself, the poet and author, Dante. He showcased Dante looking over the mayhem while also meditating on his thoughts and work at hand through his poetry. Poetry is a way to escape one's problems, but Dante uses the art form to face his fears. Rodin was able to create a sculpture that begs the viewers to face his or her own fears.

The Rodin Museum offers unique sculptures and captivating history. Walking through an artist's lifetime showcase is unlike any other experience in this world. To see what they created drives me to be a better writer. Creating is a part of who I am, so seeing what the greats created gives me a new perception of my craft. Every art form is important. We can inspire each other daily through our individual creative ideas, just like Dante's poem inspired Rodin's sculpture.

# CHAPTER 21

# FOURTH TRAVEL ARTICLE

———

## OCTOBER 1, 2021

Hello Ms. Berry,

I hope you are enjoying your downtime and recharging. You submitted three of the four articles early, which makes editing and publishing much easier on my staff.

I have great news. Now is the time to discuss your future article topics and travel. Very exciting! Your downtime ends on October 22. You'll be going to Massachusetts from November 1 thru November 25. The articles will publish in December. In 2022, I am very thrilled to tell you that you have been picked to do a few articles for our London section. Again, you are welcome to have a travel partner of your choosing.

Important Dates:

September 22–October 22: Downtime

November 1–25: Massachusetts

November 26–January 1: Downtime

January 6–February 6: London

I look forward to working with you on both assignments. Your final Paris article was just published. Congrats on a great first assignment.

Link: https://www.getawaytravelmag.com/wall-of-love

Best,
Judith Garcia
Editor in Chief
*Getaway Travel Magazine*


Good Morning,

I am doing well. I hope you are getting some well-deserved rest as well.

That's so exciting. Thank you for including a list breakdown of all the dates. It helps a ton. I have always wanted to go to Massachusetts and London. I look forward to hearing more.

Thank you for being so kind and easy to talk to during this process.

Talk soon,
Lucy Berry


## THE WALL OF LOVE IN MONTMARTRE
### TRAVEL ARTICLE #4
#### BY LUCY BERRY | PUBLISHED OCTOBER 1, 2021

The Wall of Love should be considered one of Paris's hidden gems. Located in the Jehan Rictus Garden, the wall is surrounded by beautiful greenery. The monument has been around for over twenty years and serves as a quick and peaceful tourist attraction in Montmartre year-round. Whether you are just stopping by to take a couple of photos or sitting and enjoying a quiet day in the gardens, this is the perfect place to add to your activity list. Flooded with the words "I love you," this wall adds peace to anyone's day.

*Te quiero (Spanish), mi amas vin (Esperanto), Hondgo (Hungarian), Sayo cinta ta (Malay), Ke a go rato (Sesotho), Ti voglio bene (Italian, rather for close family and friends, than lovers), Tangiuika (Mongolian), Ndagukunda (Hindi).*

Frederic Baron (Calligraphist) and Claire Kito (Mural Artist) created this forty-square-meter wall after asking people from different backgrounds how they wrote: "I love you." A simple yet powerful phrase turned into a masterpiece that is still beloved to this day. This piece of art embodies the feel of Paris and why it is called The City of Love.

## THE CITY OF LOVE OR LIGHT?

The popular debate between my best friends and me was if Paris is actually considered both the City of Love *and* Light. It was a heated debate. Ironically, Paris is attached to both phrases.

It's no secret to the average person that falling in love is a common story in Paris. There are numerous tales of proposals at the top of the Eiffel Tower and moonlit walks along the quiet city streets. I am a hopeless romantic. Therefore, I know and love the France love stories. That's not the reason so many consider Paris the City of Love. Love factors into the name, but the phrase stems from the city's beautiful architecture and skyline. You can't go five steps without running into a marvelous building, and that's the real beauty. So many new artists find their niche here. Paris is a city where dreams come true.

Paris is also known as the City of Light. At night, the city comes to life with twinkling lights, including the Eiffel Tower. Besides dazzling views with pretty lights, Paris stands as one of the first cities to install lighting in the streets. Not only were Parisians creating new ideas such as art pieces, but they also helped create the beautiful lights people see around the city.

Whether you consider Paris the City of Light or Love, we can all agree that this city brings magic to every traveler or local that graces its grounds.

# CHAPTER 22

# PARTY TIME

---

## OCTOBER 30, 2021

Two weeks ago, we met up to plan our Third Annual Halloween Birthday Bash for Aaron's twenty-sixth. Jenny, Michael, and I shifted through a ton of party ideas that could possibly top our 1980s and Scooby-Doo themes from the previous years. We decided we needed something that would blow our friends' minds and surprise Aaron on his special day. The theme had to be unique, tied to the eighties, and catered to a large group of young adults. But what could encompass all three categories and be crafted in less than a month? After consulting Google far too many times, I scrolled to the perfect idea—Plan a Murder Mystery.

Michael had knitted his brows together, interested in the theme. Jenny was intrigued and willing to throw the party together without Aaron knowing. As for me, I knew I had stumbled across a gold mine from the 1985 entertainment collection.

Jenny, Michael, and I made signs that pointed to each room in the house. There is a sign beside the stairs that reads Conservatory and Lounge, with two up arrows. Along the hallway, a sign lists the Study, Billiard Room, Library, Cellar, Ballroom, Dining Room, and Kitchen with their respective arrow directions.

Aaron and Jenny's house is lit up as the sun lights tiny pieces of the sky. It's an hour until sunset when I step out of my car. The night will be setting in as we start playing our very own live-action *Clue* game later. I smooth down my fancy baby-blue dress and try to balance on my matching heels. I wobble on my heels a little on the tiny porch steps. Jenny flings the front door open. She is in a floor-length eye-popping dark-green gown with a light-green scarf wrapped around her bare shoulders. Her hair is curled and flowing down her back. Miss Scarlet's attire really suits her frame.

Jenny says, "Oh my gosh, girl, you look stunning in blue."

"You are one to talk, girl." I whistle, "Green is definitely your color. I bet Aaron loves you in this dress."

She fans her face as we walk into the house. "Oh, I think he does."

I wobble more than walk, but I make it. "He better!" I put my hand on my hip.

"Speak of the devil," she says as Aaron rounds the corner. "There's my handsome husband, the man of the hour. Looking sharp in your suit, babe."

He pulls at his suit jacket and says, "Thanks, hon. The name's Boddy, *Mr.* Boddy."

"All right, James Bond."

He runs his fingers through his hair. There is something different about it, but I can't put my finger on it. I tilt my head and scrunch up my face. I say, "Aaron, did you do something to your hair?"

"He dyed it for tonight. Mr. Boddy has jet-black hair, while Aaron is a brunette," Jenny says. "He wanted to go all out, and I didn't hold him back."

Aaron smiles and flexes his jacket.

The doorbell rings. Jenny opens the door in one swift motion and reveals more party guests. Aaron's parents walk into the house dressed head to toe in server clothes. Mr. Sean Morgan looks dashing in his Butler suit. Mrs. Claire Morgan is breathtaking in her maid outfit as she loops her arm through her husband's.

There is someone behind them in the doorway, unsure if they should enter.

The unknown male is sporting a brown suit with a yellow bowtie. It takes my eyes a minute to recognize who is standing six feet away from me. My gears start to turn as I rack my brain. The answer almost knocks the wind out of me as the man speaks, "Hello, Lucy, long time no see."

I feel like my eyes are going to pop out of my skull. His familiar voice rings through my ears. I run my fingers over my fuzzy brown overcoat while my mouth tries to form words. A face that has haunted my dreams for a year stands in front of me, almost unchanged but somehow different, as well. His boyish smile remains as he stares at me. One hand tucked in his pocket, out of view, a nervous tick he could never hide from me. His hair is styled a different way to where it doesn't remind me of a young Justin Bieber. Is he taller? Maybe a couple of inches, but that could also be his fancy shoes lifting him up. He walks a bit closer.

Oh goodness I am not prepared for this interaction. I softly say, "Hello, David. It's been a while. The mustache and hat really threw me off."

He smooths out his over-lip decoration. "The fake 'stache will do that to ya."

"Yeah." I rub my arm. "Will you excuse me? I'm going to call Michael."

"I look forward to seeing what you have planned for tonight, Lucy."

I run out of the room. The phone clutched to my chest. I finally reach the farthest room in the house, the den. Waiting for the dial tone to stop and Michael's voice to begin feels like a lifetime. "Hey girl, I'm driving. I'm almost to Jenny's. Are you already there?"

"Him. Here. Looking dashing in a bowtie. Help. Me."

"I'm stomping on the gas now. I'm on my way. Hang in there." I hear his engine. "I am about ten minutes away. Stay where you are. Where is that?"

"I'm hiding in the den."

Fifteen minutes later, Michael appears in the doorway. He looks fancy in his gray suit jacket with suspenders peeking out, holding his dress pants up. An old-timey looking black hat with a green fabric strip around it sits on his head. He crouches down in front of me, wobbling a bit as he finds his balance. "I'm here. You aren't alone. It is going to be okay, I promise." I wrap my arms around him. I hold on for dear life.

"Thank you for coming to my rescue, boi. I appreciate it a lot. I just can't believe he actually showed up and in such an accurate Colonel Mustard costume."

"Yeah, always. I caught a glimpse of him. He did a good job on his costume." He smiles. "But, you did better on your Mrs. Peacock costume."

"You're one to talk, Mr. Green." He sits up beside me and crosses his legs. I relax a bit as I crunch my knees against my chest.

"Thrift store and Amazon shopping at its best. We should get back to the party."

I stretch my legs. "Let's blow their minds tonight, deal?" Our last two guests, Josh and Taylor, have arrived. Josh is dressed to the nines in his Professor Plum attire. He is twirling the smoking pipe between his fingers as he talks to Aaron. Taylor is beside him, looking gorgeous as Mrs. White with her little black dress and beaded clutch purse. Michael clears his throat and lets out a long, high-pitched whistle that rings through the house. Everyone's heads whip toward us from the other end of the hallway in one swift motion. We shuffle into the living room.

I motion Jenny over, and the three of us stand together in front of everyone. I focus my eyes on Aaron as I speak. "Welcome, friends. We have invited you here tonight to play a live-action game of *Clue*. Only Jenny, Michael, and I know the true ending. But, anything could happen."

I say, "Mr. Green is going to hand you your *Clue* information card. This will have what room you will be starting in and your weapon, which you will find in that room. Your card will also tell you if you are the Killer, Victim, or Pawn. Good luck. Every room in the house has a game label on the door. Now the game is up to you. Break!" I clap my hands. Everyone runs toward the rooms that are situated throughout the whole house.

I end up in the Billiard Room, formally known as Aaron's Office/Man Cave. I sit down in his rolling chair and spin until dizzy. On my last spin, I spot something shiny under his desk. I bend down and grab the shiny metal. I flip it over in my hand a couple of times. I wonder why a wrench is in here. I guess someone could have been working on one of the pieces of furniture in the last day or so. *Maybe the butler or a handyman—Mr. Boddy has plenty of money.*

A scream rings through the house.

The speaker cuts on, and Wadsworth, the Butler, says, "Everyone report to the Study. There's been a murder. Be careful. A murderer is on the loose in the mansion. Trust no one!" The speaker cuts out.

I run next door into the Study. I arrive first to find Yvette, the Maid, standing over Mr. Boddy's body with the Butler sitting at the desk by the microphone. Yvette is holding a knife and drops it the second she sees me. The blade catches the light and blinds me. As I regain my vision, everyone else comes into the room.

I point my finger at Yvette and say, "She did it! She had to have!"

Wadsworth says, "Mrs. Peacock, I am going to need you to please calm down. What is your evidence against Yvette?"

"She was the only one besides you in here when I opened the door," I say and point to Wadsworth. "Plus, she was holding a knife over Mr. Boddy and looked scared."

Yvette says, "For all we know, it could be you, Mrs. Peacock!" She picks the knife back up and points the blade at me. "You could have run in to kill him, run out, and then come back in when I discovered his body." She waves the knife around and taps her foot.

Mrs. White points to my hand and says, "If she did do the deed, then why would she leave the murder weapon in here and bring a wrench?"

Miss Scarlet says, "Bring a weapon to a screaming room, maybe?" She holds the gun at her side. "A lady needs protection, don't you agree, Wadsworth? You said, 'trust no one.'"

"Yes, ma'am," he says as he leans back in his chair, "but at this rate, we will never know who killed Mr. Boddy."

Colonel Mustard narrows his eyes at the Butler and says, "Why don't you have a weapon? You were just sitting pretty in here. What do you have to hide, sir?"

"I have nothing to hide." He crosses his feet on the desk. "I am simply the guide. I have no reason to kill my employer."

"Why would I kill our employer?" Yvette whines. "I need this job."

"No idea, ma'am, but you sure look guilty."

Before anyone can make a rebuttal, the lights go out. I hear footsteps throughout the mansion. Isn't everyone in the room? Who is covering up the murder with the darkness?

The lights come back on a few minutes later, and I am standing stock still in the Study. I am not alone. Wadsworth is still reclined behind the desk like he owns the place. Colonel Mustard and Miss Scarlet are whispering by the doorway. Mr. Green is messing with his hat, looking worried. Professor Plum and Mrs. White are looking around anxiously. I follow their eyes to the spot where Mr. Boddy's body should be lying lifeless. My eyes grow wide. Mr. Boddy's body and Yvette are missing.

Even with everyone in the room, Wadsworth reports the incident. "Mr. Boddy's supposed lifeless body is missing. Yvette is roaming somewhere in the mansion with a knife and maybe Mr. Boddy, himself. So watch your back." The voice box crackles out, and the lights blink a few times before completely going out.

A gun blasts.

Someone screams, and the voice box sends another crackle. Wadsworth clears his throat and says, "There's been *another* murder! Report to the Ballroom. Tread carefully. Anyone could be the *killer!*" The speaker cuts out, and the lights come back on.

I wobble into the Ballroom. Mr. Bobby and Yvette are lying in the middle of the room with gunshot wounds to their foreheads. The deed is done this time. Someone in the mansion is a murderer. Everyone is present except Wadsworth and Miss Scarlet.

Mrs. White says, "Where's Miss Scarlet? Does anyone see the gun?"

Professor Plum says, "Maybe she's dead?"

"All I know," I say, "is that Miss Scarlet was holding the gun when we were in the Study. Maybe she wanted to kill Mr. Boddy, and Yvette caught her. To cover her tracks, she killed Yvette, too."

Mr. Green says, "All is possible."

I shrug. "I know I didn't kill them. I don't have a gun."

Colonel Mustard points his finger at me and says, "But, you could have easily stolen it while the lights were off."

"How dare you accuse me of murder." I open my purse and show them it's empty. "I was crouched down in the hall when I heard the gunshots. Where were you?"

"I was in the Kitchen." He raises his eyebrows. "Maybe we should all be looking for Miss Scarlet, don't you think?"

I silently agree with him to move this along and find out how both the Maid and Mr. Bobby ended up with bullets in their skulls. It is all very fishy. I start with the one man who already knew them both. I make my way to the Study to talk to Wadsworth. He may not be a part of the mystery, but he definitely knows something.

As I am walking from the Ballroom to the Study, someone screams.

Two steps short of the Study, Mrs. White is covering her mouth while Professor Plum consoles her. Mr. Green looks around the corner and gasps. Colonel Mustard's eyes go hollow. I wobble to the kitchen doorway and peek around the corner. Miss Scarlet's lifeless body is lying in a pool of blood. There's a single stab wound on her side. Her skin is pale. The gun and knife are beside her.

The speaker crackles once more. Wadsworth has eyes everywhere. He says, "Another murder has occurred! Find the killer before you all meet the same fate as the three before you!" The speaker cuts out, and the hall falls silent.

"We have three murders and at least two murderers on our hands now," Professor Plum states. "Miss Scarlet was playing us the entire time."

Mr. Green says, "How so?"

Professor Plum holds up his finger. "Here's my theory. She framed Yvette in the Study. Then, the lights went out. When they came back on, both Yvette and the knife were missing. Next, someone screams when they find Mr. Boddy and Yvette murdered with bullets to their skulls in the Ballroom. Lastly, Mrs. White screams when she discovers Miss Scarlet stabbed in the kitchen. I think someone who secretly knows Miss Scarlet killed her."

"But," I say, "the only person who knew everyone was Mr. Boddy, right? He invited us here."

Wadsworth silently appears in the room and says, "You aren't entirely wrong, Mrs. Peacock. I, too, knew all of you, your secrets, and who would want Miss Scarlet quiet."

"You really do have eyes everywhere, don't you, Wadsworth?"

"That is correct, Mrs. Peacock. I know that Colonel Mustard is a murderer." He smirks and looks over at Colonel Mustard. "Should I tell them your secrets?"

Colonel Mustard says, "Wait just a minute." He takes a deep breath. "I was one of Miss Scarlet's clients, and I didn't want anyone finding out."

Mr. Green raises his voice. "You killed her to bury your secrets?"

"I had no choice." He clasps and unclasps his hands. "After seeing her shoot Mr. Boddy and Yvette, I had to do it. I never had the knife around anyone, so who would suspect me? It was the perfect plan."

"Until Wadsworth caught you." I stomp my heel and scrunch up my nose.

Wadsworth and Mr. Green rip out their badges. Wadsworth says, "Mr. Green and I are Secret Agents. Our department suspected Miss Scarlet and Colonel Mustard from the start." Wadsworth walks over to Colonel Mustard before he can run. "Put your hands behind your back. I'm going to have to take you in."

A crackling sound goes through the house, and the speaker turns on. A female voice comes over the speaker. She says, "Congratulations, you've solved the murder mystery. Colonel Mustard is the second killer, who killed the first killer, Miss Scarlet. Report to the kitchen for cake and ice cream. It is time to party."

I look into the kitchen. The pool of blood is nearly gone, and so is Miss Scarlet. The dead can hear.


I slip my heels off and wiggle my toes. The cold hardwood is refreshing. Jenny cuts the cake. I wrap my arms around her waist and lay my head on her shoulder and say, "Well, that was a successful game. But we did not plan for you to end up a victim, did we?" She picks up her game card from the table and hands it to me. I flip it over to the second side. *Killer/Victim* is printed in a huge font. Underneath, it reads: *You will frame Yvette then later kill her and Mr. Boddy with a gun.* "Would you look at that," I say, "You were both."

Jenny says, "You are probably wondering how David knew his character was supposed to kill me after stumbling in on my murdering act."

"That thought may have crossed my mind."

"Hey, David, can I see your game card?" She grabs my hand to keep me calm as he walks over to us. Almost like old times, but it will never be like that again. I focus my attention on the conversation instead of my nervous thoughts.

David gives us a toothy grin and says, "Here you go, Jen." He backs up a few paces.

"Colonel Mustard's card was a tad different. I made it that way so you and Michael wouldn't know the outcome. Anyway, enough stalling, here is what the card says. 'Killer. You will stab Miss Scarlet, so she will keep your secrets of you being her client. You will also confess the secrets in front of the other guests to keep from being humiliated by Wadsworth, who knows your secrets.'"

"So, the rooms were unknown to the killer?" I ask.

"The rooms happened naturally. It depended on where everyone was when the killer and victim ended up in the same room. As you can tell by my card, I didn't know who would kill me, which kept my movements interesting."

"Jenny here is a mastermind, don't want to make her angry." David chuckles then glances at me. "Nice job, Lucy."

I gently smile, finally feeling calm as Jenny squeezes my hand. I say, "Thanks, David. But, I couldn't have done it without my two best friends." Michael walks over and gives me a hug. "They are some of the best party planners."

"I don't know about last year's party, but the first party you planned two years ago was a blast." He messes with his hair. "But, this one was wicked interesting."

Michael says, "Our girl sure knows how to party." He sticks his hand out to David. "I'm her best friend, Michael. It's nice to see you again." They shake hands and exchange casual nods as the conversation between us dies down.

Aaron claps and says, "Wow. I really have the greatest wife and best friends ever. That was incredible." I release Jenny as Aaron walks over with his arms open wide. He wraps her in a huge bear hug. "You are the absolute best. Here's to twenty-six."

# CHAPTER 23

# DECEMBER REVEALS

---

## DECEMBER 10–15, 2021

We spent the rest of Halloween weekend talking about the *Clue* game and its bizarre ending. None of us could believe we pulled off our own mystery game. It was a good feeling. Then first thing Monday morning, I boarded a plane to Massachusetts for my first solo trip. I was heading to the hotspot of the great northeast states to write two articles for my second assignment under *Getaway Travel Magazine*. I was nervous to not only ride on a plane alone but also spend time in an unknown state by myself. I knew deep down all my friends and family were back home supporting me, which put me at ease during my travels.

I spent November exploring and learning all I could about Salem, Massachusetts's history that dates back three hundred twenty-eight years. Over the course of three and half weeks, I divided my findings into a two-piece article series. The first one focused on the horrific witch trials, and the other followed the aftermath of the town. Overall, I never had a dull moment, especially when I would FaceTime with Michael when he would ask me about all the spooky places

I had visited during the week. He was highly invested, and it made me feel safer talking to someone while walking around an unknown place.

The excitement didn't end on my trip. I didn't want to return to Alabama, but alas, I came home for Thanksgiving. It wasn't for nothing. A day after Thanksgiving, things started to change for me in the best way possible. My downtime until the new year was looking pretty bright. Two weeks have passed, and I haven't told a soul, not even my best friends.

I like this secret just being mine. No expectations. No need to impress. I am not sure if I am ready, but it is now or never.

*Besties Group Chat*

Me: Everyone ready to hit up Mellow Mushroom tonight?

Aaron: I am! I'm picking my wifey up at 4:30 to head to the restaurant.

Jenny: Okay, hubby. We are going to the Decatur location, right? I'm ready, too.

Me: Yes. It is one of the best.

Aaron: Yes, ma'am! Talk to y'all later. I am heading home.

Michael: I'm leaving right at 4:30. See y'all at 5:00, unless traffic gets me.

Me: See y'all there.

My phone buzzes with a sweet *Good luck, beautiful* text. I smile and slip my tiara ring on my ring finger. At four-thirty sharp, I head to Mellow Mushroom in Decatur. To celebrate the almost one-year anniversary of Taylor Swift's second 2020 album, I turn the volume up and jam out like there is no tomorrow. I absolutely love the sound and lyrics of this first track. I can't get enough. The opening lyrics have to be the best by far.

My twenty-minute drive was a breeze, thanks to Swift's calming lyrics. I step out into the cold December air, pull my coat tight, and adjust my gloves. I face the rare Alabama icy wind and walk across the road. I look around the street and come up empty as I reach the restaurant. I am the first one here, as always. I roll my eyes and open the heavy door. I walk up to the hostess stand and say, "Hello, can I put a name in while I am waiting for my friends to arrive?" After putting our name in, I sit on the bench and wait. I am so ready to spill my secret.

The wide double doors swing open, bringing in the cold air. Jenny comes bouncing over to me. Michael and Aaron walk up moments later. They plop down beside me and lean in real close. My phone buzzes in my hand, and it sends a tingle up my spine. Tonight's the night I'm going to tell my best friends about my mystery guy.

Jenny says, "What's got you all giddy?"

Michael teases me, "What is Ms. Lucy smiling about tonight?"

Aaron says, "What's up, Buttercup?"

"I have news." I grin and say, "And I bet none of you can guess."

"It probably includes writing," Michael guesses.

"That's one of them. But," I hold my finger up, "y'all will never guess the second one."

"Probably not, but we'll have fun trying." Aaron laughs.

The buzzer starts going crazy. Michael steals it from me and skips to the hostess stand. I roll my eyes and follow him. The waiter leads us to a booth across from the glass window that looks onto the patio. Michael and I slide in on one side while Jenny and Aaron slide in across from us.

"Okay, I need details on how you went from being scared of David at Aaron's party to having two huge secrets and being super giddy." Michael says, "How'd you go from a worrywart to giddy?"

Jenny says, "Oh, please tell us you met someone!"

"Why do you think I met someone?"

Aaron challenges Jenny and says, "Yeah, why do you think that, hon?"

"For one," Jenny says, "she is giddy and averting her eyes from looking directly at us. She has to be keeping a huge secret. Yes, bigger than writing."

Aaron smirks at me. "You can't hide anything from her."

"All right, girl, spill the beans." Michael bumps my shoulder. "Is Jenny right?"

I put my hands up in surrender. "Okay, okay, I'll tell y'all! Goodness."

Aaron motions with his hand. "Out with it."

"Okay, so, yes, the first one is about my next writing trip. In January, my solo trip to London is still on. Oh, and I met someone."

"As much as I want to hear about the London trip, I really want to know more about this someone," Jenny squeals. "How did y'all meet? Have y'all been talking much? Have y'all gone on a date? Tell us everything."

"Goodness, breathe, Jen," I calmly say. "We met on Match two weeks ago, after I got back from Massachusetts. His name is Mason Edwards. Cute, right? He is so sweet. No, we haven't gotten to go on a date yet. He is a firefighter."

"Now who needs to breathe?" She arches her eyebrows. "Also, a firefighter, I think you definitely upgraded."

I smile. "I don't like to compare people, but even without meeting him, Mason is far better than David."

Aaron says, "Does he know about David?"

"Yes, he knows about David and the divorce last year. He knows my reservations about falling too quickly and guarding my heart. He knows everything."

"He better know all the things because I want my best friend to be taken care of, ya know?"

"I know you want me to be in good hands, buddy."

"Yes, I do."

"Anyway," Michael pushes, "tell us more about him."

"Oh, you guys, he is so dreamy. Given he had to update his pictures for me, he is a real cutie." I gush. "He is a Decatur firefighter, hint at today's location. He is Scottish and a *Star Wars* fan."

"How much older is he than you?"

"A year and almost two months, June 1994 to August 1995. He's twenty-seven." My stomach tingles as I talk. I can't wait for everyone to meet each other.

"That's not bad at all. Cute, actually."

My mind drifts off as I daydream about him walking in Mellow Mushroom and sweeping me off my feet. He'll march through the doors like he owns the place, recognize me in a second, and pull me to him. Gazing into each other's eyes, we'll know we've found the one, or I could be totally wrong and a sappy, hopeless romantic.

Jenny breaks through my thoughts and says, "You want to text him, don't you?"

"Do you sniff out clues or something?" I stare at her.

"Maybe a little, but I can tell because I understand." She side-eyes Aaron. "I still do that with Aaron, and we have been together for like ever. That feeling of wanting to talk to them should never go away."

"Y'all have been together almost nine years, right?"

"It'll be nine years in February and then two years of marriage in March."

"Wow, time really flies. Doesn't it?"

"And now it is your turn to experience that for real *this time*." She winks.

"I hope so." I add, "Y'all want to meet Mason in the next few weeks?"

"Of course," all three of them say.

"When are you meeting him in person?" Michael says.

"He suggested December twentieth, so he would have time to ask off. I think it is so sweet that he wants a full uninterrupted day with me. I know it could possibly be interrupted, but it is the thought that counts."

"That's cute and very sweet of him," Jenny gushes.

"I'm just ready to officially meet him." I pause and add, "Texting can only go so far." My phone buzzes, and I smile. The rest of the world melts away.


My Little Secret: Everything went well on my end, beautiful. How did yours go?

Me: Yay. Mine went great, handsome. I should change your name in my phone, ha!

My Little Secret: Good. What is it now? I'll tell you mine if you tell me yours.

Me: You are My Little Secret in my phone. Now spill.

My Little Secret: You are Beautiful Secret in my phone. How cute?

Me: So cute. I can't wait to see what we change them to next. But, for now, my friends are staring at me. I'll text you when I get home.

My Little Secret: I can't wait either. Ha, the guys are staring at me, too.

Me: Wish I were there.

My Little Secret: Real soon, I promise. Talk soon, beautiful.

Me: Talk soon, handsome.

Michael says, "How's the boy?"

"Good, excited, and amazing."

Jenny says, "You deserve a great guy."

"I have two great guys right here." I wink.

"Though they may be great, you know what kind of guy I am talking about." She winks. "A romantic partner."

"Ah, that's the one."

Aaron gives me a serious look. He says, "So, you are meeting this guy in ten days. When do we get to meet him?"

"Hopefully during Christmas week after we meet. Depending on how everything goes. We have only briefly discussed our holiday plans."

"Y'all will discuss it as it gets closer, don't worry, Lucy Lu," Jenny assures me. "We've got your back."

"My built-in backup." I smile as we head to our cars.

I am a tad bit excited. Meeting someone is a big deal, especially for me. It was only three months ago that I was against dating. Been there, done that, wasn't interested. Then I jumped on Match, and everything changed on November twenty-sixth. Two weeks of pure bliss. I have no idea what will happen next, but I am ready.


Five days later, I am relaxing in my comfy chair, staring at my phone and daydreaming. Mason and I are meeting in person for the first time in five days. I am beyond nervous. I haven't felt like this in years. Jittery, excited, and with overwhelming emotions bubbling in my stomach, my phone buzzes on the chair arm.

MSE: I am so ready to see you. What do you think about doing a video call the night before we meet in person?

Me: Same. Like getting to see your face in real time? Yes, please.

MSE: Sunday night at six?

Me: That works for me. So, I guess I'll "see" you then.

MSE: Ha. I see what you did there. Very cute. "See" you then.

He clocks in to work, and our conversation winds down a bit. I pick my laptop up and look through my calendar again. I have downtime until the new year, but 2022 is going to be amazing. Ended 2021 with Paris, then Massachusetts, and starting 2022 with London. I could also be starting the new year with a boyfriend. Only time will tell. I stare at my Google Document. I want to write, but where are the words. I need to relax, but I also want to post a poem today or this week. A poem is long overdue. I need to focus on what I want to say. Do I write about Paris, my best friends, my new guy, or how I am moving on from my past? All great topics. I think I could somehow weave them together.

A few hours later, after what feels like forever, I copy and paste my poems onto my WordPress blog. I hit publish on my little beauties about how Paris revived my hope in everything, how I should have seen something coming, and the new feelings bubbling in my stomach. I feel good.

# Paris, My Love

Soaring confidently—
free from the shell
he trapped me in.
In Paris, the city lights
bring me to life.

My tired soul renewed.
My hope revived.
Into the great unknown, I travel.
Renewing my itch for adventure—
my greatest journey began
on the busy Paris streets.

# Waste

Hung on a Christmas tree for all to see,
but you threw the chance away
to shine for me.
You shined for someone else.

what a waste of time
you have become—
thanks for nothing.

# Safe

Safe and secure,
your embrace comforts me.
Your warmth soothes my soul
and aching bones.
Peace, hope, freedom.
I am free.

# CHAPTER 24

# UNEXPECTED

———

## DECEMBER 19–20, 2021

I sprint to the bathroom and throw on some pajamas and run my fingers through my hair. Cute but comfortable is my goal. I put on my Christmas-light pajama pants, fuzzy reindeer socks, and reindeer graphic tee. I love holiday attire. My phone buzzes with five individual texts from Mason.

MSE: I am home. I am so ready to see and talk to you, beautiful! I am almost ready to hit call. I'm getting pajama pants. Comfort is key. I'll call in a few.

I plop down in my comfy chair. As I am crossing my legs, my phone buzzes on the chair's arm. His name shows up on my screen with a request for a FaceTime call. I twist my hair around my finger and hit accept.

Mason says, "We are finally doing this." He is easy on the eyes. His eyes are emerald green like a beautiful crystal stone. His curly brown hair sits like a mop on the top of his head. A few curls fall on his forehead and bounce as he shifts.

"We are. It took us long enough," I say. "I bet I have cooler pajama pants than you." I hope he doesn't think that is dumb, but every conversation needs an icebreaker.

"Oh, I don't think you do, little lady. I'll show you mine if you show me yours." He challenges me right out of the gate—my kind of man.

I prop my knee against my chest so he can see my colorful Christmas-light pajama pants. He lifts his knee up and shows me his *Stars Wars* Christmas pants. "You went with a Christmas theme, too."

"I already noticed your reindeer shirt, but Christmas-light pajama pants, that is adorable."

I can already tell he is a genuine human being and so caring for the people around him. We are off to a good start. "This is my favorite time of year." I flip my camera to my Christmas tree. "I've had my tree up and decorated since December first." I flip the camera back to me and smile really big.

He wiggles his eyebrows and flips his camera around. "I started moving my Christmas stuff from the attic the day after Thanksgiving. You know, the day we started messaging?"

"We know how to deck the halls." I smile then add, "We will know each other a month on the twenty-sixth. How cool is that?"

He beams. "I've known you all of December. That's crazy!"

"I never thought 2021 would end like this."

"What do you mean?"

"I never thought I would go to Paris. I never thought I would stop being against getting back into dating and join a dating app. I really didn't think I would meet someone like you in such a short amount of time." My face turns beet red.

"Someone like me? Surely I can't compete with Paris?" He scratches his chin. "You went to *Paris*. I'm just me."

"You are just as good, sir." I grin. "You've helped me grow just as much as Paris did."

He moves his eyes from side to side, then looks back at me. "No, no, that's not possible. You are too sweet, Ms. Lucy."

"Oh, I know I'm sweet, Mr. Mason." I laugh. "But, I also tell the truth."

"The case is closed. I'm just as cool as Paris." He tips his invisible hat to me. "I think we have set off your giggle box, Ms. Lucy."

"I'm not complaining at all, Mr. Mason."

"Well, I'm glad you aren't because we've been talking for over an hour now."

"No way!" The minutes roll by an hour. He is so easy to laugh and talk about nonsense with. "Okay, I have a very important question."

"Shoot."

"Do you like everything Disney or just *Star Wars* movies?" This is my deal breaker. I am a huge Disney fan through and through. I hold my breath.

"You can't love one without the other, I always say." He smiles. "What about you? Are you a *Star Wars* fan, or have you only seen a few movies and or episodes?"

"Excellent point. I've seen some, but I'm not a massive fan like you. Although, I am always down to learn more."

"Did you know that learning new things is the key to a successful and healthy relationship?"

"I've been trying to tell people that for years," I exclaim. "I want a variety of likes and dislikes between me and the person I am talking to, ya know? My only want for the same is Disney because I make Disney movie and character references all the time."

"You don't want to annoy anyone, correct?"

"Finally, someone who understands."

"I'm the same way with *Star Wars*, but I can tell you'll embrace it."

"I just wanted to put mine out there, just in case. I was nervous."

"Don't be nervous to tell me things. We probably have loads in common that we can bond over and loads different that we can learn from each other."

I don't hold back. We go back and forth about interesting facts about ourselves to see if we want to keep or break our meeting for tomorrow. The stakes are high. He reveals that he is mistaken for his older brother's twin all the time. I let this dangle in the air for a moment before I challenge his music taste and dancing skills. He is smooth and laughs about me, saying we would fall if we danced together. He slides in a pickup line—maybe we can fall together. I lose it.

We could laugh together for years. I feel it in my soul. Mason Edwards isn't your typical man. He is down to earth, a family man, and calms me with his gentle smile.

He says, "I think our meeting is still on for tomorrow."

I say, "You almost said date, didn't you? I saw you hesitate for a minute. Do you want to call tomorrow a date because I kind of want to if you do?" I nervously bite my bottom lip. "Date almost sounds natural. I think we should call it a date if that is okay."

"It's a date, Ms. Lucy."

"Tomorrow night is going to be the best."

Hours effortlessly tick by with him. We move from topic to topic with ease. From Disney and *Star Wars* to family members and everything in-between. I have learned more about him in a few hours than most people in a few years. Maybe I am falling. I think everything will be fine. Tomorrow night can't come soon enough. Ice skating, food, and Christmas lights. I prop my chin on my hand and happily sigh.

His eyes grow wide. He says, "Ms. Lucy, are you okay, or is that your happy daydreaming face?"

I grin and say, "You caught me. I was daydreaming about meeting you."

He smiles. "I'm glad you still want to meet me after so many hours on the phone."

"No wonder I am starting to feel tired. Must be all the adulting."

"Adulting is an extreme sport."

"I have more time to do stuff than most, but still, everything wears me out. Afterward, I just want to lie down and listen to music on a loop."

We agree that adulting is an extreme sport and we would like to speak to a manager. We both unwind with music and are hardcore music geeks. We love all kinds of music and genres from the 1980s to now.

He says, "You know alternative rock?" He adds, "The '90s through 2000s hits from our childhood."

"Isn't 3 *Doors Down* in that genre?"

"Good catch!" he says. "I already like you. I'm awkward though, sorry."

I twirl my hair around my finger. "I already like you, too. I'm awkward as all get out, so don't worry." I muffle a yawn with the back of my hand. "I am going to go lie in bed. If I fall asleep, I'm good."

"We need our sleep for tomorrow's date, Ms. Lucy." He smiles at me. "I've been in bed this whole time."

"Ah, beat me from the get-go. Dang it." I crawl under the covers and prop my pillows up. My eyes are getting heavy. I yawn again.

"I think we should call it a night. Goodnight, Ms. Lucy. I'll see you tomorrow."

"No argument there. Goodnight, Mr. Mason. See you then."

My house falls silent. I roll over and fall asleep.

I pull into the Athens Town Center parking lot and look for Mason's truck. My eyes land on a black truck with a light tan band around the bottom of the frame. He waves. I wave back. I turn my car off, unbuckle, and step out onto the asphalt. As I'm walking over to his truck, a few spaces away, he hops out and opens the passenger door.

I walk around the back of the truck and meet him on the passenger side. He props his arm on the door and runs his fingers through his hair. He says, "For you, Ms. Lucy."

I hop up in the truck and wiggle around in the seat. "Nice truck. Messy, but nice." The console isn't too messy. It just shows that he is on the go a lot. He is either working or spending time with friends and family.

"Aren't you the observant type?" He props his elbow on the open door.

I shift my purse to the floorboard. "Oh, I am. But, it is also out in the open. Are we ready to go, sir?"

"Maybe someone can help me clean it sometime." He winks. "We are ready to go."

"Maybe someone." I laugh.

He turns out of the parking lot toward the Decatur ramp. I scroll through my playlist to find the perfect song to start our date. Finally, I found my Selena Gomez tracks in the playlist and pick a Disney song from *Tinker Bell*. "What do you think?"

"Sounds like a Disney song. I'm not sure on the movie right off, though." He merges into traffic on Highway 31.

"Well, it is a rather girly movie, so you may not know it."

"I probably do. It has just been a while since I have seen any of the girly movies." He slaps the steering wheel. "Oh, right, I haven't told you yet. I have an older brother and sister. They're twins."

"Wait, wait, wait! You have older siblings who are twins, but you get mistaken for your brother's twin?"

"Joshua and I look more alike than he and Emma do." He shrugs. "I guess it is a guy thing. I'm not sure."

"Do y'all look more like your mom or dad?"

"Joshua and I are younger versions of our dad, while Emma favors more of our mom. She has a sprinkling of Dad, whereas we had a tiny bit of Mom."

"By favoring your dad like your brother, you tend to look more like him than your sister does."

"Uh, you pick up fast." He smiles. "I bet you don't know where we are going to eat, though."

I look out the window. I see at least a dozen restaurants around us. "I bet it is somewhere not too fancy but feels fancy, you know?"

"This restaurant is like that, not too fancy, at all. Just right in my opinion." He makes a left onto a narrow road. "We are almost there."

"Are we going to Applebee's? Because it is my favorite non-fancy restaurant." He turns into their parking lot seconds later. "No way! No way! Mason, you didn't?" I bounce in my seat.

"I did! I did!" He throws the truck in park and unbuckles. He shifts to look at me. "I try to pay attention the best I can. I love surprises." I unbuckle my seatbelt and reach for the door handle. "No, no, I've got your door, Ms. Lucy."

I pull my hand back. "Yes, sir, I could get used to this."

Twenty minutes later, we are at our table with our meals in front of us. Everything looks and smells so good. I am more concerned with getting to know him than stuffing my face. Not that I am shy, but I am ready to ask and answer tough questions. My stomach growls and cuts through the silence. He stares at me. I gulp. His eyes are sparkling in the overhead lamp's dim light. He is slightly smiling while rubbing his hands together. He waits for my response as I continue to stay silent. I take a bite of my steak to calm my nerves.

"Question time," Mason says. "Where do you see yourself in five years?"

"A tough one right out of the gate," I say. "I'm married with a little family that includes two kids and a dog. I want either two girls, or a boy and a girl. I think an Australian shepherd puppy would be a lot of fun."

"The girl has big dreams. That's a tough one to follow." He takes a deep breath. "In five years, I'm married with a family. I want a little boy. Having a girl would be interesting but so worth it. I want a dog that's my pal." He takes a bite of his food.

That's cute. He's cute. Oh no, I'm in trouble.

He tilts his head at me. "What are you thinking about so hard?"

I debate on whether or not I should tell him. I take a deep breath and say, "I'm crushing hard on you, sir."

"I'm crushing hard on you, too, ma'am." He reaches across the table and holds my hand. He runs his thumb over my palm and smiles at me.

"How in the world is this possible?" I stare at my hand in his. Except for him helping me out of the truck, this is the first time he has held my hand. I am over the moon right now. I don't know how to process what is going on in front of me.

"We seem to fit together so well. I can't believe it. You make me smile and laugh at random things. You enjoy the simple parts of life but love to dream big. You are incredible."

I bring his hand to my cheek and rest it there. "You have definitely surprised me, Mason Scott. I can't believe I am on a date with you. I just want to keep spending time with you."

He arches his eyebrows. "Using my middle name. I like that. I just want to keep spending time with you, too, Lucy Matilda. Did I mention how much I like your middle name?"

"I like yours, so it is only fair that you like mine." I tease him as the waitress refills our drinks and drops off our bill.

He only breaks away to check the amount, grab his debit card, and use the machine to pay for our meal. He puts away his card and holds my hand again. "Are you ready to go skating for a little bit before we go see some Christmas lights?" He slides out of the booth and then helps me out.

Thirty minutes later, he parks in front of Decatur Ice. He looks over at me and says, "Let's do this." Before I can say anything, he hops out of the truck and the freezing wind hits my face. He runs around the front and opens my door. "My lady." He holds out his hand to me.

We debate over skate sizes, the most difficult task in my opinion. He surprises me with his sports background. During elementary school, he played soccer and learned a little bit of hockey. Although, I thought he played both soccer and football growing up. I was wrong. He stopped playing soccer in middle school and joined the football team at the beginning of his freshmen year. He is a gentle jock, not your stereotypical rom-com athlete. A movie where he would have a love story with the head cheerleader. This isn't a rom-com, and I'm not a cheerleader, but we have rom-com aspects brewing.

We step onto the smooth ice. I grip his hand as we start to skate around the perimeter. I say, "We are still standing. That's a good sign." I watch all the people around the rink skating almost effortlessly. I wish I looked that good, but I know I look like I have chicken legs. A girl learning how to walk in high heels for the first time. A baby calf walking after birth.

He says, "Standing for right now." He wobbles a bit. He places his hand on the small of my back to steady us.

"You have a little bit of skating history. We'll be okay."

"From like fifteen years ago!"

"Have you not been skating for fun in all those years?"

"Off and on, but not as much as I would like. You know, going into burning buildings takes up a lot of time." He grins.

I roll my eyes. We make the first loop around the rink. I try to speed up a little and drag him with me. I epically fail and start to wobble. He catches my back just in time. "Ah! That was a close one." I take a deep breath. "My heart is beating so fast."

"I bet it is." He suddenly stops us. He faces me and puts his forehead to mine, and whispers, "I'll always catch you."

Our mouths are so close, but I don't dare make a move first. I'm not sure if I am ready. Am I?

He moves closer and whispers again. "Can I kiss you or should I wait?"

"Can we wait until we are dating? I think we will, so I want to wait. Is that okay with you?"

His eyes sparkle, and his face softens. "Whatever you want, Ms. Lucy."

I whisper, "That's my number one want. I want to be sure this time around. Will you wait for me?"

"I've waited a lifetime, so it seems, to feel like I do right now. So, yes, I'll wait for as long as you need me to."

"To clarify, we are just going on dates. You'll have to ask me to officially be your girlfriend. Deal?" I grin. I know the wait will be worth it.

"Deal." He smiles and grips my hand tighter. "What do you say we warm up with some hot chocolate on our way to the Christmas lights?"

"You are speaking my language." I back away from him and look at him. I am one lucky girl. "You are the best." I pull him to the rink's exit before he can say anything else. I want my hot chocolate. The cold air is setting in, and I am freezing. I unlace my skates and skip over to the counter to turn them in. He returns my shoes, and I tap my foot as Mason finally exchanges his and slips them on his feet. "Ready?" I finish adjusting the heels of my sneakers.

"Ready!" He laces his fingers through mine. "We are going to have so much fun."

The wind hits my face. "Brr!"

A perfect end to a perfect first date with hot chocolates in the cup holders, Christmas music playing, and Christmas lights. I look out the window at the pretty twinkling lights and blow-up displays in the neighborhood. This is my favorite time of year, the season of giving.

There is no other place I would rather be than beside Mason. He squeezes my hand as he slowly guides his truck down the neighborhood streets. This takes the cake as the best start to Christmas week. What a way to end 2021. I can't wait to see what is next for us.

I hope we end up together.

# EPILOGUE

———

## ONE YEAR LATER

I fling the front door open to reveal his beautiful smile behind a bouquet of red roses. He wraps his arms around me and tightly squeezes me. We break apart, and he hands me the flowers. I skip off to find a vase in one of my many kitchen cabinets. I say, "Are you coming or not, Mason Scott?" I rummage through the bottom cabinets.

"I'm coming. I'm coming." His sneakers smack the hardwood floor. Seconds later, he pops his head in the doorway. "Looking for a vase rather fast this time, are we?"

"My sunflowers died within a day, and I don't want it to happen again. Do you know what today is?"

"We don't want that. Why do you think I brought you roses? We are celebrating something special today, babe."

I smile. Him calling me babe never gets old. "We went on our first date a year ago today, babe."

"I got you twelve roses and a thirteenth one that will never die, like our love. Can you find the fake one?"

"You are just so thoughtful." I throw my arms around him. I kiss his nose, then his cheeks, and last his lips. He pulls me in closer, and we kiss deeply. We melt into each other so effortlessly. I pull away. "Our guests will be here any minute now, silly boy."

"I'm your silly boy, and you're my silly girl." He leans back in and presses his nose into my neck.

"Forever and always." I wrap my arms around his neck, and he breaks away to look at me.

"Forever and always sounds wonderful." He quickly throws his arms around my waist and lifts me up. I squeal and bend my legs. He murmurs into my shoulder, "Hmm, I love you, Lucy Matilda."

I pull back as he sets me on the floor. "I love you, too, Mason Scott."

I jump plum out of my skin as someone loudly knocks three times on the front door. I bury my face in his shoulder and take deep breaths. He rubs small circles on my back. "It's okay. It's just someone at the door." He puts me at arm's length. "Want to go let them in?" He holds both my hands, brings them up to his lips, and kisses them.

I melt as his lips brush against my hands. "Okay, but will you hold my hand and walk with me? Greet them together?"

He stands by my side and smiles. "Let's go."

Jenny is sporting a blush pink maternity dress with an off-white fabric headband. She is glowing. Aaron looks nice in his light pink polo and khakis. Jenny runs up and gives me a side hug. "We're having a girl, Lucy Lu. We found out today, so you know we had to sport some pink tonight."

"Pink suits y'all!" I bounce a little and squeeze her shoulder.

Aaron says, "She's glowing." He stares at her like no one else is around him. He comes back to reality a few seconds later and bumps fists with Mason. "Hey, dude. It's been a while."

I shut the front door. We shuffle into the living room as we chat and rave about life. Mason says, "Been busy fighting fires, training newbies, and taking this beautiful woman out on dates. You know, the normal things." He bumps fists with Aaron again. "Let's go sit down and talk. I think Lucy said everyone should be here around six. Y'all were just a tad early."

"We are early everywhere," Aaron says. "I bet Jenny will go into labor early."

"Knowing you two, probably so." I laugh. "I want to be there, so I better get a text."

"Oh, you'll get one," Jenny assures me.

Mason says, "We'll be the first ones there, for sure, Jen." I smile at him as he gushes over Jenny's baby news. I wonder if he is thinking about our future. Soon, we'll be celebrating our one-year anniversary. I hope there are many more to come.

"Aww, thank you, Mason. I am really glad she has you. I know our girl is taken care of."

"I'll always take care of her." He grins at me. "I couldn't ask for better."

I bump his shoulder and smile. I ask Jenny, "Oh, what's your due date?"

"A little over two months after our anniversary. She's due on May twenty-third." She rubs her belly.

A knock interrupts our conversation. I skip to the front door and fling it open. Mr. Michael Sparks is dressed in all-black besides his favorite blood-red shoes. He says, "I'm ready to party with my favorite people. Are you?"

"I'm always ready, boi!" I pull him into a hug. "I missed you. It's been too long," I say into his shoulder.

He puts me at arm's length. "It has only been like two weeks, if that, Lucy." He shakes his head. Some things never change.

"Two weeks too long. What's new?"

"I am officially self-publishing my first horror poetry collection on January first."

Jenny exclaims, "No way!"

He looks around me at Jenny. "Way!"

A few hours later, my house is filled to the brim with family and friends. I am content. In a few weeks, Mason and I will be leaving for my next writing assignment. I wanted to have a party before we left, and it turned out fantastic.

After grabbing a slice of cheese from the party platter in the kitchen, I head back to the living room to join the party. I walk in, and my five favorite guys are standing in the middle of the room whispering. I give Jenny a look, who is sitting on the couch beside my nanny and mom. They all just grinned at me.

Before I can reach the center of the room, with the Christmas tree in the background, Mason kneels on one knee. He opens the ring box and says, "Lucy Matilda Berry, will you make me the happiest man in the world and marry me?"

I cover my mouth. I inch closer to him as everything around us melts away. "Yes, of course. I would love to be your wife, Mason Scott Edwards."

He slips the engagement ring on my finger. He swoops me up into a hug and yells, "She said yes!"


**Email from Judith Garcia [Sent December 21, 2022 / Read Again January 4, 2023]**

Hello Ms. Berry,

I hope this email finds you doing well and enjoying the holidays. I can't wait to read more writing from you in the New Year.

On January 4, 2023, you will be leaving for your next writing assignment and will be back on February 4.

Discussed Articles Topics:

- Hollywood Studios
- Disney Dining Experiences
- Disney is for All Ages

*Be aware that these articles can change at any time. You can tweak the specific topics if you run into problems.

Have a safe trip when you leave in the new year. We'll be in touch.

Best,
Judith Garcia
Editor in Chief
*Getaway Travel Magazine*

I stare at my ring as I scan over my editor's email a zillion more times. We stand in line for the plane for Orlando, Florida. I say, "Am I really getting to write about the best vacation spot ever?" I feel like I am going to get shushed like we are in the library, but alas, no one pays any attention to my outburst.

Mason wraps his arms around my waist and says, "You are, my dear."

# ACKNOWLEDGMENTS

———

Thank you to everyone who has been with me through my writing journey from *Will You Love Me Again?* to *Where Will We Go?* As much as I wish I could take on everything and anything by myself, I couldn't have done this without my support system. Thank y'all for sticking with me through all the struggles, tears, successful days, and huge milestones. I am so blessed to have y'all on this journey with me. I will never be able to thank you enough for helping me fulfill my childhood dreams.

A special thanks to my family, fiancé, and friends for believing in me every step of the way.

First and foremost, I want to thank my Nanny. From the first moment she held me to the last day I held her hand, she always saw me for me. She believed in my stories and my words before I did. Saving every poem and rough draft I gave her, she loved and devoured it all. Nanny was my first reader for both of my books and the first one to know the ending for *Where Will We Go?* Her love and guidance are what kept me pushing forward on this uphill battle of a writing journey. I knew as long as I had her, I could do anything. I dedicated this book to her in honor of all our memories and the impact she left on my writing. She's my guardian angel. I'll love her forever.

Thank you to my parents for putting up with all the publishing costs, my bad moods, and changes while supporting my author journey. I appreciate y'all more than y'all will ever know. Momma and Daddy, I love y'all so much. I'll never be able to thank you enough for your support and patience while helping get my writing career off the ground.

Thank you to my fiancé, who entered my life at the perfect time in September 2020. I was knee-deep in writer's block while writing *Where Will We Go?* and the second he walked into my life, everything changed. Dustin Hooie, you are my better half, a partner in crime, my rant listener, and my biggest cheerleader. I don't know what this book would have been without you. Thank you for being the Mason Edwards to my Lucy Berry. I love you forever and always.

Thank you to Stone Parker for not only being the Michael Sparks to my Lucy but for being my best friend for nearly six years. Thank you for loving me through every part of my life. A special thank you for writing my Author Biography and Michael Spark's poetry. I love you, boi!

Thank you to Mark Stenberg and the Study Break Magazine Staff for putting me in a remarkable group of writers in 2018. Because of that internship, I met Elizabeth Invanecky and Haley Newlin. Thank you to Elizabeth and Haley for believing in my writing and this book even when I lost my spirit. I am so thankful that we reconnected in 2019/2020. A special thanks to y'all for introducing me to the Creator Institute and New Degree Press. Although this year hasn't been the best, I kept pushing forward to create a great book for my readers and especially in memory of my Nanny. With the help of the Professors, Author Coaches, Editors (writing/

publishing sides), and publishing team, I was able to publish my second book. It was a struggle, but looking back, I am so thankful I didn't give up on this opportunity. Thank you for understanding my vision and helping me reach even more book lovers.

Lastly, I want to say thank you to everyone who has encouraged me in any way possible during my writing journey. It means the world to me to have so many people in my corner. A special thank you to my author community for preordering and donating to my presale campaign. Thank you for believing in my story before anyone else. I couldn't have done this without y'all.

Savannah Bearden

Elizabeth Invanecky

Jessica Schmidt

Whitney Schrimsher

Cody Dunnavant

Jennifer & Chris Craig**

Carol Yee

Dustin Hooie**

Debbie Coulter

Cassidy Fairbanks

Isaiah Ray*

David Adams

Lisa McLaurin

Jennifer & Conner Partridge

Tammy & Paul Casteel

Thomas Rhodes*

Leahgrace Simons

Tracey Casteel

Terry & Cathy Lamar

Kailey Bright*

Jessika Ruck

Haley Haggermaker

Amy & Howard Waston

Donna McCart

Vicky Askew

Roxann Allen

Haley Newlin

Lentia & Trey Winn

Rachael & Sean Lamar

Reilly Vore

Emily Bennett

Chris Hooie

Shanda Craig

Eric Koester

Jake & Allee Casteel

Stone Parker

Rylee Fletcher

Kelley Cornelius

Caitlyn C

Amanda Hooie

Tammy Griffin*

Brandon Posivak

Crystal Morse

Gwenda Pepper

Kayla & Zane Griffin

Emily Riddle

Frank Anderson**

Kristin Beccatti

Amanda Wilson

Eric Garner

Paulette Fletcher

Vicky Phillips

Sal Gallaher

Zach Chastain*

Anyston Belt

Briana & Caleb McConnell

Dalton Smith*

David & Debbie Kieff

Marge & Tony Pack

Brianna Mason

Leah Osborn Harper*

Holly & Wayne Hardiman

Jess Avalos

Ambre Stark

Susan Black DeBerardinis*

Zach Sherrell

Aaron Winn*

Jessica & Brandon Pepper*

Butch Pettus

Sarah & Eddie Eggler

Michelle Casteel

Haley Kirby

Mary Jo Ramsey

Sandra White

Zeke Sherrell

Melissa & Danny Kieff

Lindsay Craig*

** = extra donations or multiple copies purchased

* = WYLMA Package